SHIMMER

In Miami Beach, all hell is breaking loose. First, a swimmer makes a gruesome discovery, and then the city is rocked by an explosion. Detective Sam Becket has a vicious killer to find, and his only lead is a local who's seen a frightening stranger: a young man, silver from head to toe, shimmering in the night. But nothing can prepare Sam for what the killer has in store...

Hilary Norman titles available from Severn House Large Print

LAST RUN
RALPH'S CHILDREN

SHIMMER

Hilary Norman

Severn House Large Print
London & New York

This first large print edition published 2010
in Great Britain and the USA by
SEVERN HOUSE PUBLISHERS LTD of
9-15 High Street, Sutton, Surrey, SM1 1DF.
First world regular print edition published 2009 by
Severn House Publishers Ltd., London and New York.

British Library Cataloguing in Publication Data

Norman, Hilary.
   Shimmer. -- (Sam Becket mysteries)
   1. Becket, Sam (Fictitious character)--Fiction.
   2. Police--Florida--Miami--Fiction. 3. Detective and
   mystery stories. 4. Large type books.
   I. Title II. Series
   823.9'14-dc22

   ISBN-13: 978-0-7278-7874-8

Severn House Publishers support The Forest Stewardship
Council [FSC], the leading international forest certification
organisation. All our titles that are printed on Greenpeace-
approved FSC-certified paper carry the FSC logo.

Mixed Sources
Product group from well-managed
forests and other controlled sources
www.fsc.org Cert no. SA-COC-1565
© 1996 Forest Stewardship Council

Printed and bound in Great Britain by the
MPG Books Group, Bodmin, Cornwall.

For Anita Kern

ACKNOWLEDGEMENTS

My gratitude goes to the following: Howard Barmad; Jennifer Bloch; Batya Brykman; Sara Fisher, whose help and support I will sorely miss; Isaac and Evelyne Hasson; huge thanks yet again to Special Agent Paul Marcus and to Julie Marcus (the *almost* real Sam and Grace); Bella Patel; Helmut Pesch; Sebastian Ritscher; Helen Rose (for so *very* much, always); Rainer Schumacher; Dr Jonathan Tarlow, for seafaring expertise again, as well as medical. And, as always, for being a technical wiz, helping with research, and for just about everything else, Jonathan.

The Epistle of Cal the Hater

'Lie down,' Jewel tells me.

I tell her I don't want to lie down.

'Do it,' Jewel says, her voice real hard, like her name.

So I do.

Because the alternative is worse.

Because she'll find other ways to hurt me.

And she won't love me any more.

It's been happening for such a long time.

I've learned a lot over time. I've learned that I can shut down my mind to bad things, and that I can survive, no matter what. But I've also learned that when you lock away bad stuff in your mind, worse stuff happens. Because all the pain and humiliation and hate you've ground down and buried starts festering like pus on the root of a tooth, or even maggots on a corpse. And sometimes it comes oozing out one tiny worm at a time, but other times it just stays in there, expanding and building up inside you until you blow.

Cause and effect, which I've read about.

Stands to reason.

But that effect is real bad, and I know it. Bad enough to make me hate myself.

Which may, I think, be worse than anything.

Cal liked to write, always had. And to read. He chose the word *'epistle'* for his private writing, even though he'd looked it up in his Merriam-Webster Dictionary and seen it was a word for a letter, and this was not a letter as such because he wasn't writing it *to* anyone, but on the other hand it wasn't a journal either, it was just his *writing*. The first definition in the dictionary said it was a letter in the New Testament, but he already knew that because he knew the Bible pretty well, knew that the word was repeated over and over – the Epistles of the Apostles – and Cal liked the way that sounded, and even now it clicked regularly into his mind and he found himself saying it out loud like a tongue twister –

'The Epistles of the Apostles, The Epistles of the Apostles...'

Sometimes he'd even sing it and do a kind of little tap dance to the rhythm, which used to worry him in case he was maybe being sacrilegious, because he did respect the Bible and going to church, but on the other hand he'd learned by now that there wasn't any point in worrying about playing around with a *word*, because Lord knew he'd done things far worse.

'I am sacrilegious,' he'd written in his Epistle, 'and I know it, and it scares the crap out of me because I know it means that hell's waiting for me at the end of my time, but there's nothing I can think of to change that, and I reckon it's not really my fault, is it?

'None of it.'

1

June 6

South Beach, like a thousand other beaches around dawn, felt and looked almost born again, a whole new world creeping out of the dark, eons away from its strident, semi-pagan late-night self.

Even with the din of music shut off, Ocean Drive was never silent, never seemed entirely at rest. The restaurants and bars were closed, the last Thursday night into Friday morning revellers had gone to their groggy beds, takings had been locked away, waiters and bartenders had soaked their aching feet and crashed; yet even now there were early morning drivers moving slowly up and down the street, a lone jogger down on the beach, his long hair swinging with each bounce, two roller bladers skimming along the promenade, a middle-aged woman walking her dog on the grass, a sleeper stirring nearby, disturbed for a few moments by the growl of the sanitation truck cleaning the gutters and moving slowly onwards.

The morning was warm and humid, no freshness to it, the remnants of last night's thunderstorm still grumbling to the east somewhere in the greyish violet-to-pink-tinted sky, but the beach itself was serene, all primal innocence. The shallow Atlantic waters moved gently, peaceably, the smooth sands, shifted overnight by birds and breezes and rain and other, unseen forces, seemed almost to be posing for the moment in soft beige and pastel hues, taking its rest before people returned again to tread and soil and taint.

Like all beaches in Miami-Dade County, South Beach had rules imposed upon it, a list of prohibitions posted along the promenade and beach. No alcoholic beverages permitted, no glass containers, no walking on the dunes. No animals, no firearms or fireworks and more besides.

No 'rough and injurious activities'.

Which rule scarcely *began* to cover what Joe Myerson had happened upon in the midst of his Friday sunrise swim.

A regular dawn swimmer, Joe cherished this time.

'If I ever drown or have a heart attack or just get eaten by a goddamned fish while I'm out there,' he once told his brother, 'you'll know I went happy.'

Finished now, his almost private ocean-Eden mornings.

Never again.

It had seemed, at first glance, nothing more interesting than a stray rowboat, pink-painted but shabby, bobbing on the calm morning waters.

Joe had noticed it from a hundred or so yards off and felt an instant tug of curiosity; not just because it looked out of place on South Beach, but because even crumby old rowboats were generally kept tied up or beached, and for some reason it occurred to him that it might not be empty after all, that there might be someone inside the boat, someone he couldn't see, someone sick, maybe, lying down.

Lying down, for sure, but way past sick.

Which was more than could be said for Joe.

Worst thing he'd ever seen in his life.

Ever hoped *not* to see again.

'Mr Myerson dragged it ashore himself,' Neal Peterson – one of the Miami Beach

11

Police Department patrol officers first on the scene – told Detectives Sam Becket and Alejandro Martinez when they arrived a few minutes after eight.

On the beach, right across from Ocean Drive and 10th Street, less than a handful of blocks from their own office on Washington Avenue.

Fruits of evil just around the corner.

The crime scene team had beaten them to it, were already busy around the rowboat inside the cordoned off area.

Peterson had known these two detectives for a long while, knew how tight the bond was between Becket, the tall, rangy African-American and Martinez, the shorter, much slighter but, on occasions, tougher Cuban-American.

'There was a length of tow rope tied to the bow which looks hacked off,' the patrolman went on. 'Mr Myerson said soon as he saw the victim, he wanted to get the hell away, but he knew he'd never forgive himself if the boat drifted out too far or maybe capsized.'

'Poor guy.' Sam looked towards the row-boat, then out to sea.

'More guts than most,' said Peterson.

'A prince,' said Martinez, who seldom took anything or anyone at face value. 'Where is he?'

Peterson turned and indicated his partner, presently standing over a figure hunched on the sand about thirty yards away. 'He has some scrapes on his arms from dragging the boat.'

'Are we sure that's what caused them?' asked Sam.

'Doc Sanders seems to think so,' the officer said. 'He took some swabs, dressed the scrapes. No stitches needed.' He paused. 'Nothing that looks like he might have been in a fight, nothing like that.'

'He knows he's going to have to talk to us?' Sam checked.

It was a kind of lottery in the Violent Crimes department as to who got named lead investigator in any new case, and Sam had been handed this one by Sergeant Alvarez, which mostly meant that back in the office he'd be the one burdened with the report writing and lion's share of the paperwork. With so many years of informal partnership between them, neither Sam nor Martinez made any big leadership distinctions while they were out in the field.

'Yes, sir,' Peterson answered Sam's question. 'He said he didn't mind waiting, said he can't see himself getting down to work any time soon.'

Another figure in shirtsleeves, familiar, overweight but not lumbering, was moving over the sand towards the detectives, ducking under the yellow crime scene tape. Dr Elliot Sanders, the medical examiner, slipping a surgical mask down from his nose and mouth, lighting up a cigarette as he came close.

Nicotine – and good whisky, off-duty – always a priority with Sanders.

'Bad one,' he said right away, his round, expressive face and keen eyes displaying grim distaste.

'Is there any other kind?' Sam said.

The ME shrugged. 'Asian male,' he said. 'Indian, maybe. Early twenties, though it's a little hard to be sure of much.' He glanced at Sam, who covered well on the whole, but tended towards a queasy response to the remains of violent death. 'The guy was strangled, but he's a real mess.' He fished in his pocket, brought out two more masks, handed them over. 'Just in case.'

'Of what?' asked Sam.

'Some kind of chemical involved.' Sanders took a pull on his cigarette, stubbed it out on the sand, then picked up the butt and dropped it in his trouser pocket. 'Body's almost certainly been washed, maybe hosed down or sluiced off in the ocean, but there's still quite an odour, so as I said, just in case.'

They donned gloves and shoe covers and walked together, all stepping carefully over the sand, even though they already knew that this area of beach was unlikely to have been the scene of the actual killing.

'Holy fuck,' Martinez said, catching first

14

sight of the victim.

'What the hell happened to him?' Sam had to force himself to keep looking.

The victim was naked, all the visible skin from his face down to his feet striated in raw, bloody, almost burned-looking lines, some diagonal, others vertical, a few criss-crossing. Anything that might have helped ID him was gone; he wore no watch, no rings – a band of paler skin around his wrist spoke of a medium-size round-faced watch, but there was no such mark on his wedding band finger or any other, so he was perhaps unmarried, and though his hands, like the rest of him, were wounded, his nails were well kept.

The detectives could smell it too. Not intense, but evident nevertheless, like a mix of salt water and the chemical that Sanders had mentioned.

'Smells like Clorox,' Martinez said.

'Could be,' Sanders agreed. 'But it might be something more corrosive.'

Sam was crouching now, the mask over his nose and mouth, staring down at the strange lines of wounds, observing that while some looked straight and almost systematic, others were more jagged, more random looking, more crazed.

'They use some kind of rake?' he asked.

'Possibly,' the ME said. 'Though my first guess would be something more like a scrubbing brush, heavy duty, maybe even wire. More later.'

'But this didn't happen here,' Sam said.

'Certainly not here,' Sanders confirmed, 'nor in the boat, I'd say.'

'And I guess you can't say when,' Sam said.

These were things he wished he'd never learned. About the many complications involved in the estimating of time of death, about the variables that influenced rigor mortis and body cooling, and Sam, to his regret, did not need the ME to tell him that he would not be using a thermometer until he'd been able to examine the victim for evidence of sexual interference; and that in any case, body temperature was likely to mislead in a case like this, where the body had been moved after death, possibly dunked in the ocean before being placed in a new location – namely the rowboat – then left for an unknown length of time to the mercy of the elements.

'You guess right,' Sanders said. 'It'll be a while.'

'You believe Myerson's story, Doc?' Martinez asked.

'Innocent bystander, if I'm any judge,' Sanders said. 'Shocked, a little excited, maybe. Not a suspect.'

Sam and Martinez both figured the ME for a pretty good judge.

The interior of the boat was grimy, with no

16

visible traces of blood or bleach or any other chemical, which was bad news on one hand, indicating an absence of evidence, but at least it also meant no spillage or contamination problems – at least not here on South Beach, so no apparent reason to keep the beach closed once the crime scene team were through.

Sam was eyeing the victim's neck. 'Some kind of ligature?'

'Uh-huh,' Sanders said. 'Some fibres there, look like cotton. The killer probably came at him from behind.'

'And all this...' Sam scanned the dead man's other wounds. 'Before or after death, would you say?'

'After,' Sanders replied. 'Almost certainly.'

'Small fucking mercy,' said Al Martinez.

2

Except for Joshua, her nine-month-old baby son, and Woody – the wire-haired dachshund-miniature schnauzer cross she and Sam had rescued almost four years ago – Grace Lucca Becket was home alone on the West Island in the Town of Bay Harbor Islands, when the doorbell chimed just after nine a.m.

She came out of the nursery as the dog began barking and went to the hall window that gave the best vantage point over the front door step.

Claudia Brownley, standing on the path down below, wearing a blue denim trouser suit, the jacket slung over one arm, two travel bags on the ground behind her, looked up and waved.

'I don't believe it!'

With a cry of startled delight, Grace ran down the stairs and flung open the door and her arms, and her sister stepped into her embrace, leaning against her, while Woody did his best to clamber up Claudia's legs.

'Woody, get down.' Grace drew back and regarded the bags on the path, which were much too large for a weekend visit, even an extended one. 'Sis, what's going on?'

Claudia lived with her husband Daniel Brownley and their two sons, Mike and Robbie, thousands of miles away, on Bainbridge Island in Washington State, a ferry ride from Seattle. It was not her habit, neither was it practical, to show up unexpectedly on her sister and brother-in-law's doorstep.

'Don't I get to come in?' Claudia asked.

'Oh, God, of *course*, come in.' Grace seized her in another swift, warm embrace, then picked up one of the bags while her sister heaved up the other, and they came inside together, dumped the bags in the narrow

18

hallway and headed straight for the kitchen.

It was the heart of this small house and always had been, even before Sam had entered Grace's life, before they had married and adopted their daughter Cathy, long before they'd had their son.

'So,' Claudia said, staying in the doorway, 'where's my nephew?'

'Sleeping,' Grace said. 'I hope.'

In a perfectly run world, she supposed, her son ought to be awake, but for the past several nights he had been waking at erratic times, and his thirty-eight-year-old mom and forty-one-year-old dad were both feeling the strain.

'Can I just look at him?' Claudia begged.

'I want to look at you first,' Grace said.

'I'd rather you didn't,' Claudia said. 'I look lousy.'

'You look beautiful,' Grace said, which was true, except that she'd also instantly observed that her sister had lost several pounds and gained some lines around her brown eyes. 'I'm the wreck,' she added, pointing to her own hastily pulled on chinos and sleeveless white blouse.

There were few physical similarities between these two sisters. Grace had inherited their late mother Ellen's Scandinavian colouring, and Claudia had Frank Lucca's dark hair and eyes and pale olive skin – those outward details mercifully her only obvious

19

genetic legacy from their father, she and Grace had long since agreed.

'Come on.' Grace gave in, took Claudia's hand and drew her up the stairs and into the nursery, a small, charming room decorated in pale blues and piled with soft toys.

'Oh, Grace,' Claudia whispered. 'He just gets more wonderful.'

Which Joshua Jude Becket undeniably did, this baby boy whose cheeks were the colour of cappuccino, dimpling whenever he smiled; who had been born in the midst of mayhem and tragedy, but who was now, thankfully, a sturdy, healthy bundle of frequently lusty and inquisitive contentment.

His aunt stroked his dark hair, her touch delicate. 'I won't wake him.'

'Just for a little while longer,' Grace whispered back, gratefully. 'Which will give us a chance to be just us.' She laid an arm around her sister's narrow shoulders. 'I can't believe you're here.'

She was experiencing, if truth were told, somewhat mixed feelings about the suddenness of Claudia's arrival. Without question she felt a most overwhelming sense of gladness at having her sister here with her again – but she knew too that she might, if asked in advance, have hesitated momentarily because she was in the throes of organizing her return to work, with all its complications, and all that following a period of minor post-natal depression.

'Plus a little post-traumatic stress,' her father-in-law had diagnosed some months back.

Dr David Becket was Sam's adoptive dad, a sixty-three-year-old Caucasian Jew who measured, these days, no more than five-nine ('shrinking all the time,' he claimed), but whose six-foot-three son still looked up to and trusted him above all men in the world. A man of wisdom and humour and great kindness, and infinitely more of a father to Grace than her own had ever been. And even if he was a paediatrician, not a psychiatrist, and on the brink of full retirement, David Becket was still the medic Grace would most listen to even if she'd had the chiefs of Mount Sinai *and* Jackson Memorial on hand to advise her.

'You're entitled,' he'd told her when she'd first confessed her sense of inadequacy to him. 'And you're not alone,' he'd added. 'It's hard to be joyful or even optimistic when two young people in your family are grieving.'

Yet still she'd felt shame for feeling bleak and not completely in control at exactly the time when she ought to have been filled with gratitude and competence. Even if she, more than most – being a psychologist herself, albeit a practitioner of child and adolescent psychology – knew better than that. *Ought* to

21

know better.

Different when it was the shrink suffering the blues.

She had mixed feelings now, too, for an entirely separate reason. Because for months now she'd been worrying about Claudia, knowing that all was not as it should be with her, had even, a few times, decided it was high time she packed up Joshua and flew to Seattle with him – and Sam would have backed her up, no question, but each time she'd thought about it, Grace had found reasons not to go. And now here Claudia was, without so much as a warning call, with two large bags. And, more to the point, a husband and two sons back home.

Something was very wrong.

3

The investigation was underway.

The rowboat and victim having been photographed and checked over as thoroughly as possible in situ, the body – still in the boat – had been covered and removed from the scene, and was on its way to the medical examiner's office, where every fraction of an inch of the small vessel would be examined for evidence – after which Sanders would begin his painstaking work on the deceased himself.

The skills of the ME and his team were their best chance for a swift resolution in this case, Becket and Martinez were well aware, with no true crime scene to pore over. Any trace evidence turned up by the officers and technicians on the beach would almost certainly be either totally unconnected with the crime, or might be linked to Joe Myerson, the man without whom – as Sam had told him earlier – it was possible the crime might never have been discovered.

'I guess he'd have washed up someplace,' Myerson had said.

'Not necessarily,' Sam said. 'With more weather on the way.'

The guy had looked a little better for a moment after that, and then he'd remembered what he'd seen.

It would be a long time till he forgot that.

4

It wasn't easy getting much out of Claudia.

She had asked, soon after her arrival, if she could stay for a while.

'Sure you can,' Grace had said. 'You know that.'

Managing, with an effort, not to ask why.

'Dan's going to work from home,' Claudia said. 'Take care of the boys.'

'Can he do that, with the office to run?' Grace asked, since Claudia worked part-time in her husband's architectural practice these days.

'Don't you think I'm entitled to a break?'

That wasn't like Claudia at all, that kind of self-pitying snap-back, and Grace had decided it was time to delve, but then Joshua had noisily woken up, which meant that the next hour or so had been all about him. And seeing Claudia holding her nephew close, seeing her tenderness and the little boy's happy responses, Grace felt once again over-poweringly and unequivocally glad that she was here.

This was the sister who had often clung to her for comfort after Frank Lucca, their father, had abused her, who'd followed her lead when Grace, the younger sister, had discovered her own inner strength and masterminded their escape from Chicago to Florida. The sister who had always been close, loving and absolutely necessary to her.

It was hard for Grace to imagine what might have gone wrong in the Brownley household, because for as long as Claudia, Daniel and the boys had lived down in the Florida Keys, all had seemed about as bliss-ful as any family scene could be. But then

24

Daniel had made his decision to move all the way north-west to Washington State, had set up a shiny new architectural practice in Seattle and found his family a great waterfront house on Bainbridge Island, a thirty-five minute ferry hop from the city (and a location once picked by CNN and *Money Magazine* as the second-best place to live in the United States).

The waterfront position had been intended to make them feel at home, and Grace's impression had been that it had certainly worked out for Daniel and the boys. But not so well for Claudia, which Grace had suspected for a long time.

And done nothing about it. Not that there was much she could have done, except make her regular phone calls to ask how her sister was doing, and, of course, worry about her.

Now, a new heap of guilt came flying at Grace. She'd been too busy with her own life to consider Claudia properly, too busy with her own family and her patients – and then all hell had broken loose almost a year ago, after which they'd been blessed with Joshua, and ever since then it had all been about learning to cope with motherhood and her own new, unfamiliar uncertainty.

Excuses.

'You can stay as long as you want,' she told her sister now.

She couldn't believe she hadn't said exactly that right away.

'Only I thought,' Claudia said, 'with Cathy away, there might be space.'

Cathy, their beleaguered daughter, who'd gone through more pain and grief in her young life than most people endured in a whole lifetime, and who had told Grace and Sam a little over three months ago that she was going to do some travelling because there were too many bad memories for her, on campus at Trent University and at home and on the beach and just about every place she looked in and around Miami.

'And I know it's all going to come with me wherever I go,' Cathy had told her parents, 'but still, I have this feeling that getting away for a while might help me.'

Sam had fought it longer than Grace, wanting passionately for their daughter to stay home and let them go on helping her heal, but his wife had reminded him that maybe home was getting a little claustrophobic these days for a twenty-one-year-old with a need for private space to howl out her pain.

'Not to mention having a paranoid cop for a dad,' David Becket had added, 'wanting to mount surveillance every time Cathy comes within a mile of anyone who *might* spell trouble for her sometime in the next three decades.'

'Am I really that bad?' Sam had asked his father.

'You just want her safe,' David had said. 'We all do, son.'

And Cathy's travel plans had sounded safe and well thought through, and even if she had needed their permission they'd have known they had to let her go, because whether or not it worked out for her, that was the only way they could hope to get her back again when she was ready to come home.

So for now, Cathy was on the West Coast, working as a coach's aide at a Sacramento college, after which she was scheduled to work and train at a series of summer athletics camps in various parts of California.

And every time Grace opened one of her kitchen cabinets, she saw a box of her daughter's favourite Honey Graham Life cereal and missed her more than ever.

But Cathy's bedroom was available for Claudia.

5

The area canvass was already well underway, a small team of detectives working through every residential, hotel and commercial building with an outlook on to Ocean Drive between 5th and 15th Streets, as well as the promenade, dunes and the beach itself, checking every available surveillance camera, their aim to speak to every resident, worker, proprietor and visitor in the vicinity.

'Let's hit the Strand first,' Sam had said at the outset, since that particular boutique hotel faced the beach between 10th and 11th Streets, and was also one of the few buildings in that part of the Art Deco District with balconies – and a rooftop known as one of the best spots in South Beach for watching firework displays.

And maybe homicides, too.

Nothing there, nor at the Victor, no one discovered anyplace as yet with anything useful to talk to them about, though in the circumstances neither Sam nor Martinez had expected this to be easy.

'Mildred wants to talk to you, Sam,' Detective Beth Riley informed him at around eleven as she and Mary Cutter – a petite, attractive detective with whom Al Martinez had enjoyed a brief, but pleasurable relationship some years back – came into the large office shared by the Violent Crime detectives.

Sam's antennae were up. 'Where and when?'

'Usual time and place, she said,' Cutter answered.

Which meant around noon in Lummus Park, on a palm-shaded bench.

'Think she has something?' Martinez asked.

There was no acrimony between himself and Cutter, though fear of just that was what had driven them both to ending the relationship before they'd got in too deep. No special woman in Martinez's life these days, though that was, he claimed, the way he liked it; no one to worry about night and day, he said, no one to fear for him.

'She didn't say,' Cutter answered.

Homeless people were often high on the investigators' agenda, seldom as suspects, more often just the most likely bystanders to have stumbled on potential evidence or useful information.

Mildred Bleeker was a bag lady of uncertain years who enjoyed a relationship of mutual respect with some of the cops and

29

detectives in the Miami Beach Police Department. In return for their courtesy – and, now and again, a bottle of Manischewitz Concord Grape – Mildred had never shown any great qualms about assisting the police with occasional nuggets of information about crimes of violence, especially those related to drugs.

She did, however, have her preferences, and for a while her favourite had been a young patrolman named Pete Valdez, but he'd left the department a few months ago, and since then Mildred's personal bias had leaned firmly towards Sam.

'I heard about your troubles, Detective Becket,' she'd told him one morning last March, encountering him on the corner of Lincoln and Washington and accepting his invitation to dip into the bag of Krispy Kremes he was bringing to a departmental meeting. 'I hope you don't mind if I ask you how your family are faring now?'

'I don't mind at all.' Sam had been surprised but touched, had told her they were faring pretty well, and then he had shown her some photographs of Joshua, and in return Mildred had tugged out a gold locket from beneath layers of mostly black clothing – she always wore black with just a few splashes of colour – and had opened it to reveal a pair of tiny black-and-white photographs of a young man and woman.

30

'My fiancé,' she had said.

'And you,' Sam had said.

'About a thousand years ago,' she said.

'I'd still know you anywhere,' Sam told her. 'Handsome couple.'

'Donny was one of a kind,' Mildred said. 'They broke the mould, you know?'

'Same with my wife,' Sam said. 'Grace.'

They'd left it there, respecting each other's privacy, but there had been a fair number of exchanges since, and during one Mildred had confided that Donny had died as an innocent bystander in a drug-fuelled shooting. Sam had tried a few times to persuade her to come eat with him in a restaurant or coffee shop or even back at their house, which Grace had encouraged – anything that might take the lady's fancy – but she had always thanked Sam and refused. So far as he could tell, Mildred Bleeker's lifestyle was of her choosing, and the closest they'd ever come to lunching in comfort had been a couple of conch-filled tamales on her bench.

There was no reason to think that Mildred's message was in any way connected to the killing, Sam realized now.

'Could be anything,' he said, as Cutter set down a coffee cup on her desk and Riley started checking her messages.

'Mildred know about the rowboat?' Martinez asked.

'She didn't say,' Riley said, raking one hand through her short red hair, her mind already half on other things.

'Guess she wouldn't,' Martinez said. 'You not being Sam Becket.'

All Sam knew was that he'd give a whole lot more than a dozen tamales for so much as a clue as to where the slaying had taken place. With nothing new to go on, and with the likelihood that the brutality had gone down *inside* someplace – maybe in a motel or hotel room or a brothel or a garage or some-one's private apartment – the only way they were going to find out about that any time soon was if it was some place where, say, an employee had walked in this morning to find more than they'd bargained for.

No reports yet of bloodstains or chemical spillage or even struggle.

Sam was itching to see Mildred.

6

Grace was sometimes afraid that Cathy might never come back.

Too many things she'd seemed fearful of since Joshua's birth.

'Which is not really like me,' she'd told Magda Shrike a few months back. Magda being her former mentor and psychologist and good friend who'd relocated to San Francisco for a time, then returned a year ago. 'Or never used to be.'

'Events take their toll,' Magda had said. 'On everyone.'

'Except the bad things last year hardly happened to me, did they?'

'They happened to people you love, so of course they happened to you,' Magda said. 'You're being way too hard on yourself, Grace.'

Which was one of the reasons Grace had decided, a while back, that it was high time she went back to doing what she was best at. Namely thinking of others, specifically her patients. The children she could be helping.

Plenty more psychologists on the beach.

True enough, but still, it was what Grace had spent years training for and many more years than that practising, and she was good at her work, she was too honest to deny that much.

Except that she'd also been having to come to terms with the fact that returning to practice would mean having to find someone to help out again; not exactly a replacement for Lucia Busseto, her former office manager – because frankly, Grace could not imagine ever again feeling able to entrust her young patients' confidential files to any other person.

I'd be entrusting Joshua *to another person.*

That thought struck fear into her again now, as it always did when she and Sam discussed getting any kind of help in the house.

Which was, in itself, she thought, not entirely healthy.

'Beeba,' Joshua said from his high chair in the kitchen, right on cue.

'You said it,' Grace answered.

David and Saul – Sam's twenty-two-year-old adoptive brother – had both offered to take care of Joshua any number of times, and Lord knew she and Sam would trust either of them to the ends of the earth. But this was not so much babysitting as a long-term lifestyle decision, one that she was going to have to come to terms with as determinedly as any other working mom.

Still, right now, Claudia was here. Had flown thousands of miles because apparently she needed her sister, and whether that was for shelter or a shoulder to cry on, or for something else entirely, then Grace knew it was time to give herself a sharp kick in the rear and simply be here for her.

Sam called at eleven thirty to tell Grace he was on a new homicide investigation.

Which meant, as she knew, there was no telling when he'd make it home.

'We have a visitor,' she said.

Claudia was upstairs, settling herself in

Cathy's room, and Grace had called their daughter in Sacramento a half-hour ago, and Cathy had assured her that she had no problem with that.

'I like thinking of my room being used,' she said.

'Want us to take in a lodger?' Grace asked, deliberately light.

'I wouldn't go that far,' Cathy said, sounding merry, then sent them all hugs, especially Joshua who she said she was missing like crazy and could not *wait* to see again, all of which had made Grace feel a whole lot better.

She told Sam now about how Claudia was looking.

'Something's definitely not right with her.'

'You've known that for a while,' Sam said. 'And it's good she's come to you.'

'Even if it might mean she's walked out on Daniel and the boys?'

'Especially if that's what's happened,' Sam said. 'No one better than you to help her fix things.'

'You think?' Grace was wry.

'I know,' Sam said in his deep, rich voice.

Nice to have a husband with such faith in her.

Grace wished she could feel as certain.

35

7

Not a day went by when Sam did not remember how lucky he was to have his family, to be *alive* and free and still a Miami Beach detective.

It might all have been so different. He might have lost his job or worse, but the investigators into last year's nightmare had accepted that Cathy's life had been in immediate danger, and Sam's punishment for acting out of his jurisdiction and worse besides had been decided by a discipline committee of Majors and Captains, and he had been suspended for eighty hours. He might have been demoted or even transferred out of the Detective Bureau. As it was, he was still doing what he loved.

Even if sometimes – on a day like this one – that love seemed a little bizarre.

'So,' Martinez said to him just after noon as they walked down 11th towards Ocean Drive, Sam holding a bag containing two Cuban sandwiches and a bottle of Manischewitz for Mildred, his own Starbucks cup of Tazo iced tea balanced in his other hand.

'Your gut telling you anything useful yet?'

'Not a damned thing,' Sam said.

'Mine neither,' said Martinez.

The only thing that had come out of Sanders' office to date was confirmation that the tiny threads he'd found in the strangulation indentations were white cotton, the kind you'd find in the cords of mass-produced towelling robes.

'Common as shit,' Martinez had said.

Which was why they'd been reduced to trying to zero in on their own gut reactions out here on the hot, humid South Beach streets, asking themselves the usual questions.

'So, OK' – Sam went first as they crossed over Collins – 'what do we figure happened to our John Doe?'

'Not a domestic,' Martinez said. 'Not marital, at least.'

'Robbery gone bad?' Sam said, since rage, they'd learned through experience, could be triggered by almost anything, and for all they knew, their victim might have been a rich guy with a wad in his wallet and a diamond-studded Rolex on his wrist.

Before person or persons unknown had strangled the life out of him, brutally raked his flesh and then poured a still unidentified chemical all over his wounds.

'Drugs or sex or both,' Sam said.

'Sex,' Martinez chose. 'Gay encounter

gone bad.'

The destruction of body and face spoke of deep, raging violence, and the detectives had learned from experience that murders with a homosexual element could sometimes be unusually violent.

'The strangling aside,' Sam went on as they turned right on to Ocean Drive, 'this was an assault on his skin.'

The music was already thumping out of the restaurants, pretty waitresses standing on the sidewalk peddling their wares, proffering menus and cut-price lunches.

'But *after* death,' Martinez said, 'which speaks against sadism.'

'Could be race then,' Sam said.

Race crimes made him depressed as well as sickened.

'Race and sex,' his partner said. 'Who the fuck knows?'

'We're supposed to know,' said Sam.

Mildred was not hungry.

The news on the streets that a man was horribly dead had killed her appetite.

'I apologize,' she told Sam, when he offered her a sandwich.

It was just the two of them, Martinez having returned to the office. For safety's sake and common sense, the detectives rarely went anywhere alone, but there were exceptions to the rule, and Mildred was such a one. For one thing, she was trusted, and for another, if she did have some significant information, they knew she was less likely to pass it over as uninhibitedly if Sam was accompanied.

'Nothing personal,' she had told Martinez once, when he'd come along with Sam to meet her. 'I just have this *thing* for Detective Becket, you understand.' She had winked then, her sharp blue eyes knowing, and her lined, weather-beaten face had crinkled with her smile, and Martinez had taken a chance and kissed her age-spotted hand, and Mildred had laughed and seemed pleased enough, but then she'd still waited for Martinez to take off anyway.

There was something stately about the lady, Sam had thought as he'd approached their usual rendezvous and seen her, a hostess waiting for her guest, sitting surrounded by her worldly goods on the palm-shaded turquoise-painted bench near the children's play area not far from Ocean Drive and 6th Street. This was her patch, the place where she slept at night, held court for the privileged few, and though Sam had caught occasional glimpses of her on Washington Avenue and on the beach itself, he had no idea where she spent the rest of her days.

She invited him to sit, turned down the sandwich, but accepted the wine. Sam knew better than to suggest she keep the Cuban for later, because it was June and the cheese and ham and butter would be rancid in no time without refrigeration, and Mildred Bleeker, he knew, had standards.

'May I offer you a drink, Samuel?'

Since Judy Becket, his adoptive mom, had passed away, no one else in the world had called him that, but Mildred believed that names from the good book should never be messed with, had reminded him that his late parents had chosen it for a reason.

Now she held out the bottle, label facing out, almost like a wine waiter in a fine restaurant. It was a ritual she seemed to enjoy, even though Mildred knew perfectly well that Sam would decline because he was on duty.

He thanked her as always, raised his cardboard cup of tea.

Time was, Sam Becket had been a real coffee aficionado, had been pretty much addicted to fine espresso, but one of the after-effects of last year's traumas was that he doubted if he'd ever be able to so much as sip coffee again.

'So,' he said now, peaceably. 'Is this purely social?'

'You know I wouldn't waste your time, Samuel,' Mildred said. 'Especially not when you have such serious work to do.'

'I wish that weren't so.' Frankly, homicide aside, Sam could think of any number of worse ways to while away an hour than talking to this lady. 'And before I forget, Grace sends her best.'

She and Grace had never met, but they knew about each other, and Grace had told Sam she suspected she'd enjoy the experience if they did have the opportunity.

'And mine to her,' Mildred said.

Sam took a sip of his tea, waited a moment.

'So what's up?'

'That poor man, of course,' she said.

'Mildred, did you see something?' Sam came right to it.

'I'm not a witness to the crime, thank the Lord.' There were people around, lazing on the grass behind them, strolling on the promenade and, beyond, on the beach, but no one was close enough to hear her, yet still Mildred lowered her voice. 'And what I have seen – *who* I have seen – most likely had nothing at all to do with it.'

'Try me,' Sam said, gently.

'I saw a stranger,' she said. 'Someone new.'

Mildred spoke slowly, thoughtfully, and though she had been mulling this over at length, it went against her principles to pack trouble on to someone else's shoulders when they might not be in the least deserving of it.

'Now I know, same as you, this place is always filled with strangers – and I use that word advisedly, Detective – but this young

41

man just gave me a bad feeling.' She screwed up her face, wrinkling her nose so that for a moment she looked almost pug-like. 'And I'm hoping it wasn't just his appearance, because I try not to set store by that kind of thing.'

'I know that,' Sam said.

Mildred shook her head, her salt-and-pepper hair long but pinned up tidily – and Sam had never seen it otherwise, had often admired that as well as the lady's ability, against all the odds, to keep herself clean-smelling. 'He was nothing more than a boy, really, and maybe just another poor soul selling himself to keep from joining the likes of me on the streets. But still, there was something about him that made the skin on my back creep, and it was a whole lot more than the way he was done up.'

'How exactly was that?' Sam was intrigued.

'He was...' She gave a small shrug. 'He was *silver*, all over. But not exactly flashy, he was more delicate than that; more like mother-of-pearl or the scales of a fish.' Mildred nodded. 'That's what I thought to myself, at first: that he was like some gorgeous silver-scaled dead fish on a slab in the super-market.'

Sam waited until a man, wheeling a trolley half-filled with coconuts, had passed them by. 'His clothes were all silver?'

'Everything was silver,' she said. 'From his

42

hair all the way down to his toes – he had those terrible shoes that make people look like they're walking up on the mezzanine instead of the first floor, you know?'

'Sure, I know.' Sam smiled, because listening to Mildred Bleeker was often a pleasure in itself; and he'd have been interested in knowing if she'd received her education from some fine school, or if perhaps she'd been self-taught, but since Mildred wasn't one to speak much about herself, chances were he'd never find out.

She shook her head again. 'But then I realized he wasn't a bit like a dead fish, because this boy was all life, all movement. He was more like some beautiful dragonfly, shimmering in the night, and I wanted to smile because he looked so *good*, almost like a skinny angel without wings, but instead my heart started thumping and I got these goosebumps.'

'Did you see his face?' asked Sam.

'I did,' Mildred answered, 'and that was silver, too, but that aside, I couldn't tell you anything much that would distinguish him from any other skinny young man, though he looked...'

Sam waited a moment. 'What? He looked at you? Did he see you, Mildred?'

'He did not look at me at all, Detective. He was too inside *himself* to do that, I thought.' She smiled. 'He seemed to me like a young man ought to look in the midst of love-making.'

'In the midst,' Sam asked, 'or at the height?' Which was the most genteel way he could think of to try to ascertain if the stranger might have been climaxing, just possibly because of what he might recently have done, or have been about to do, to their John Doe.

'You mean was he having an orgasm?' Mildred grinned. 'No, sir, not yet. But he was most certainly having a heck of a time.'

'Was he high, so far as you could tell?'

'I don't know,' Mildred replied. 'I'd say not, but of course I had no way of knowing that for sure.'

'So where was this? And when?'

Down to business.

'Not last night,' Mildred said. 'It was early yesterday morning, around two a.m.' She wore two wristwatches, one with a pale blue band on the right, one appearing to be gold, old and tarnished, a narrow bracelet with a small face, on her left wrist. She had told Sam in the past that she valued punctuality. She was, he had found, a reliable witness.

Early Thursday morning. His happy demeanour not likely, therefore, to be immediately connected to the homicide. Unless he had already been planning the crime and relishing the anticipation.

Probably just a stranger.

'And where did you see him?' Sam asked.

'On the promenade,' Mildred said. 'Just along from here, near 7th.'

Three blocks from where the rowboat had been pulled ashore.

It could – almost certainly did – mean nothing, and they both knew it, except that Mildred Bleeker was not given to seeing psychos around every corner.

This afternoon, with South Beach alive and pulsing, people out and about enjoying themselves in the hot, muggy sunshine, ignoring building clouds and forecasts of more thunder and rain, it was hard to picture silver oddballs high on possible dreams of murder.

But Mildred was nobody's fool.

'I asked myself afterwards,' she said, 'and then again this morning, when it kept coming back to me: why exactly did he make me feel so afraid?'

'Did you find an answer?' Sam asked.

'I did,' Mildred replied with certainty. 'He made me feel that way because I realized it wasn't just any ordinary skinny angel he put me in mind of, wings or not.'

Sam knew before she said the next words.

'He put me in mind,' Mildred went on, 'of the angel of death.'

Sam looked down at her beside him on the bench, a surge of protectiveness sweeping him. She was a small woman, no more than five foot one, and most probably, he thought, slightly built beneath the layers of clothing.

'We're going to be putting on extra patrols in the area,' he told her, 'for the next few nights at least, but I'm not sure I like the idea of you staying out here alone.'

Mildred looked up at him. 'Planning on arresting me, Samuel?'

'No, ma'am,' he said.

'This is my home.' She gestured around them, at the grass and trees and the sandy promenade and dunes and the beach beyond. 'This is my freedom.'

'I know that,' Sam said.

'I can't endure walls,' Mildred said. 'Not since Donny.'

She had said as much before, though never expanding on it, and Sam had no reason not to believe her, nor the slightest wish to disrupt her, let alone cause her distress.

'Would you do me one favour?' he asked.

'If I can.'

'If I give you a cell phone with my numbers programmed into it, will you promise to use it?'

'You mean if I see him again?' Mildred asked.

'And if you're ever scared again,' Sam said.

She smiled again. 'Where am I supposed to charge this thing?'

Nobody's fool, Mildred.

'I could get it charged up at the office,'

46

Sam said.

'I wouldn't be using it much, I guess,' Mildred said.

'We could arrange to pick it up every few days.'

'That would mean you'd be having to know where I am.'

'It would,' Sam agreed. 'Sometimes.'

Mildred thought for another moment.

'I think,' she said, 'I could live with that, Samuel.'

8

'I wish,' Grace said, towards evening, 'you'd tell me what's happened.'

'I told you,' Claudia said. 'I needed a break.'

'And?'

'And I wanted to see my sister and her family.'

'And we're happy to see you,' Grace said. 'Or Sam would be if he were here.'

The baby was asleep up in the nursery, and they were back in the kitchen. Outside, the storm that had been threatening all afternoon was blowing the palms and flowers and soaking the land, but in here an aromatic fish stew was simmering on the stove, and the sisters were at the big old oak table, sipping a good red Chianti and eating olives. Other than the playpen in one corner and the toys scattered around the room – and the doggy door installed last year after Woody had developed a bladder problem – little had changed in here since Claudia's last visit. It was still a room with a rustic, homely feel, warm wood and copper pans, comfortable, richly woven cushions on the chairs and family photographs on the walls.

It was just the two of them this evening, with Sam working on the new case; and Grace had been thinking of asking David and Saul to join them – Friday evenings were often family nights in the Becket household, with Jewish Sabbath candles being lit, a custom Sam had loved ever since David and Judy Becket had plucked him, aged seven, out of tragedy and adopted him – but then she'd figured that would have given Claudia the perfect excuse not to open up, and if there was anything Grace was certain of, it was that her sister needed to do exactly that.

They'd both showered and changed a while ago, Grace into a long pale blue cotton T-shirt, Claudia into a comfortable tan linen dress, her bare feet with pale-polished nails, exactly matching her fingernails (Grace could barely remember the last time she'd even thought of giving herself a pedicure), tucked beneath her on her chair.

'We used to share things,' Grace said. 'Good and bad.'

'We still do,' Claudia said. 'Just not everything.'

'Of course not,' Grace said.

Claudia took a long sip of wine.

'I can't help,' Grace said, 'if you won't talk to me.'

'I can't talk to you,' Claudia said, 'until I'm ready.'

'OK,' Grace said. 'We have time.'

Claudia set down her glass on the table, uncoiled her feet from beneath her, set them down on the floor, sat up straighter.

'I've screwed up,' she said. 'Big time.'

Grace did not speak.

'My life is a mess, and it's totally my own doing,' Claudia went on. 'And I know I can tell you just about anything, and I know I have no right to keep secrets when I've just shown up without so much as a by-your-leave on your doorstep—'

'You have every right to your privacy,' Grace said.

'Spoken like a shrink,' Claudia said dryly.

'I'm sorry.'

'Maybe a shrink's what I need,' Claudia said.

'Me too,' said Grace, and was rewarded by a ghost of a smile.

'But not tonight,' Claudia said.

9

June 7

At three o'clock on Saturday morning, after the storm had moved away, leaving bright sprinkles of starlight in the night sky, Cal was holed up in his room.

All he could afford right now, these few lousy square feet in a fleabag.

Not even a *real* fleabag. A room offered for cash and no complaints in return for no questions asked, by a guy who worked in a bed and breakfast on 11th Street; except this 'room', this lousy pit at the back of a derelict building in a dirty no-name alleyway behind Collins, with no hot water and a toilet which only flushed one out of every four times, wouldn't have passed a health check as sleeping quarters for a goddamned rat, and Cal hated it, but he couldn't afford to care too much so long as the guy kept his word and left him in peace.

So far, so good, and Cal knew the sonofa-bitch would have no cause to complain, because Cal liked things clean, took care of himself, found it hard to bear dirt or stink around him, and he'd bet that this scuzzy room had never been this close to hygienic in its whole pitiful existence.

He did hate it. He wanted to be on his boat, but he couldn't risk being there, at least for now. *Baby*, his Baja cruiser, was old and undeniably shabby, but the motor was OK and it was all he'd been able to afford and it was, at least, his own, and he felt great, horny as hell, riding the waves on it, loved taking care of it – and it was killing him not to be able to go back right now and eradicate any lingering traces of what had gone on there early yesterday morning. But the waters around Miami Beach were patrolled at night at the best of times for drug smugglers and illegals, and now was definitely *not* the best of times.

He knew he was doing the right thing, staying here for now in this pit of anonymity, and in a day or two he'd be able to go check out *Baby*, maybe not go too close first time, but try to gauge when it might be safe to go back. Out in the bay or on the ocean he'd be too exposed, and in the small marina where she was moored he'd feel too hemmed in and at risk if they came for him. At least on dry land he could run if he had to, blend in with the crowd, become invisible.

Invisibility went against the grain for Cal, but right now it was what he needed.

51

What he would most like to be doing this very instant was to be outside doing his *thing*. What he did best. Namely reeling one in and then fucking him or her before getting paid for a good job well done. And it was well done, and those who had experienced it knew it, because Cal was no ordinary hustler, Cal was the original *joy*-boy.

So this was such a waste of a good night, because even if he wasn't fucking, he could still be out just walking his walk. The one that made him feel *so* good. The one that made them notice him.

It was hard work putting together his night look, took hours sometimes, but the time and effort were worth it just for the way they looked at him.

His potential customers. His johns.

More than just regular johns, sometimes. And then, oh Jesus, the *thrill* of it. Whether they were hurting him or it was the other way around, the buzz-burn of it consumed him.

He liked it better, mind, when it *was* the other way around. He was no freak, he preferred hurting them.

Bestowing pain.

He had written a few times in his Epistle about self-hate, but he knew that was really a crock, because he enjoyed telling lies when he wrote, liked changing his style and voices and mixing up truth with artful fabrications, so that sometimes when he looked back on it, even he couldn't quite remember what was real and what was not.

The whole guilt thing was something Jewel had taught him, something he knew how to whip himself into, and that could almost be fun, too, drinking gin and getting so far down on yourself that you figured you were on your way to damnation.

Cal had always liked sex. All kinds.

It had taken him a long while to find out that there was something even better.

He knew that now, though.

10

It was twenty to four when Sam got home.

First thing he did, after letting Woody say hi to him, was go upstairs to take a look at Joshua, and the only good thing about being as bone-weary as Sam was right now was not having to fight the temptation to pick up his baby boy for a cuddle, because he was frankly afraid he might drop him.

Not too many dads, mercifully for them, had quite so much awareness of the agonizing ramifications of fleeting carelessness around small children. His first son, Sampson Becket, had been lost to him and his first wife, Althea, after just two years of life, killed by a drunk driver, a senseless accident that had happened sixteen years ago but would go on haunting Sam forever.

He looked down now at this beautiful new miracle given to him and Grace, and pure love buffeted him like a great wave.

'Daddy's home, son,' he murmured, bending to touch two fingers to the soft dark hair on Joshua's head. 'Sleep sweetly.'

He turned and went next door, where the other great love of his life was sleeping too. He locked away his gun and holster, then draped his jacket over the back of an armchair in one corner, dumped the rest of his clothes on the seat, padded barefoot into the bathroom to brush his teeth and barely refrained from groaning with sheer relief when he finally slipped beneath the covers.

Grace stirred anyway, reached for him, and Sam dragged his head off the pillow to kiss her. 'Sorry,' he whispered. 'Go back to sleep.'

'Did you see Claudia?' she asked.

'Gracie, it's almost four,' he said.

'I tried getting her to talk.'

'No go?' Sam said with an effort, but already on the way down.

'Not yet,' Grace said. 'Any luck with the new case?'

'Not so's you'd notice,' he said.

'Sleep then,' she said.

He was there before her.

11

Cal could not sleep.

He could not get past the need to be out there again on the street, making out like he was a part of the late-night freak show. He didn't mind them thinking he was one of them – unless it was someone like that old bagwoman he'd seen on the promenade a couple of nights back.

He'd felt her checking him out with her snoopy old eyes, which had made him mad because she was nothing but an old bottle-baby-bum with no right looking at him and judging. But that was what they did, the lowest of the low; they looked at other people like they thought they were superior, like they had special dispensation, special *rights*...

She was probably out there again right now, free as a stinky, mangy bird, while he was on lockdown in this damned cell of a room.

Not near as bad as a real jail cell.

Few things as bad as prison or even juvey.

Jail had been a break from Jewel, but that was all that had been good about it. All that wickedness stealing around corners, oozing at you out of the night, flicking like snakes' tongues through cell doors; and sometimes the awareness of that had turned Cal on, but mostly being locked away with the chicken hawks and baby rapers and *them* had scared the bones of him.

He'd got his tattoo in jail, had written about it later in the Epistle.

Turned out to be one of the things that made me their target.

Them. The ones Jewel taught me to hate.

The screwy irony of the tattoo is that I only paid for the goddamned thing because I thought it would be a nice gift for her. White cross in a red circle with a blood drop in the middle, all nice and neat, just over my heart. But Jewel went ape-shit when I showed her, said that what that symbol stood for on my white skin was not only that I was a racist, but a horse's backside too, because now I'd turned myself into target practice for them.

'Might as well hold up an invitation over your dolt head,' she said. 'Ask those egg plants to come and beat those shit-for-brains out of you.'

Jewel has a nice turn of phrase on

occasions, knows just how to make a man feel real good about himself.

One day, I expect one of them may do what she said.

It's hard to know how much I'll care.

Maybe I'll even welcome it.

My life, after all, being a little less than a fine thing.

The thing he had done just over twenty-four hours ago was still singing in his blood.

If he were to share that feeling with any-one, they'd probably think him some kind of fiend, which he was not.

Though he had done it once before.

Caused a death.

He hadn't *meant* to that time, not at all. But he had been picked up by a woman in Wilmington, North Carolina – not too far from where he'd bought *Baby*, as a matter of fact, and his other pal, too, Daisy, his sweet tandem bicycle and the *best* trick-tease machine – and they'd been fucking, and she'd gotten so excited that her heart had friggin *stopped.* And that had freaked him out some, because sure she'd been older, but she was still a woman, and if he'd been with some old guy he'd have known it was a risk, but this had been a tribulation he hadn't bargained for at all.

It had happened at her town house, and lucky for him there'd been no niceties before the sex. Not even a drink offered, just straight in through her elegant front door and into her fancy bedroom, so that the only things Cal had touched – other than her – had been her sheets and pillows. So after it happened he went and found himself a pair of rubber gloves in her kitchen and changed the bed linen – Pratesi, they'd been labelled, he remembered the name along with how good the sheets had felt against his skin, *mega*bucks without a doubt, though Christ knew that hadn't helped her at the end, had it? He'd been careful as hell about removing his condom and wiping over her body with a damp towel, and he was still thankful, long after, that she hadn't wanted to kiss him and had turned down any kind of oral sex. She'd paid him generously in advance, so he hadn't had to risk taking cash from her Louis Vuitton wallet – and he might, of course, have robbed her blind at that stage, but he was no common thief, and the only thing he had taken away from that house, aside from the gloves and stained bed linen, had been a bottle of Rest-Ezee tablets he'd found in the back of her bathroom cabinet, because he'd been having trouble sleeping, and this woman wasn't going to be needing them any more, that was for sure.

He'd only begun stressing *after* he'd left Wilmington about how he was bound to have left behind some microscopic traces of himself, because that was when it came back to him that the cops probably had his DNA on their files, so even though it hadn't been his fault that the woman had died, it had made him paranoid for a long time after. But no one had come looking for him either on *Baby* or in any of the places he'd moored her, so after a while he'd stopped fretting and had decided that maybe she'd had a husband who hadn't liked the idea of other people knowing that his wife went out looking to pay for her jollies.

And Cal figured that he had, at least, given her a happy exit.

It had changed him, though.

Cal had come to believe that people who'd never actually presided over the death of another human being could not begin to understand how it felt. And that was how it had felt to him – as if he'd been somehow in charge – because even though it had been her body's fault, not his, he had still been inside her when it had happened, so he was, in a sense, responsible for it, which was, when all was said and done, pretty damned impressive.

Not as impressive as what had happened early Friday morning.

His heart hadn't stopped until after the cord had choked off his breath and finished his life. But after that part was over, some-

59

thing entirely different had overcome Cal. A rage totally unprecedented for him, part of it directed at the dead man for being what he was to begin with – one of *them* – part at himself for wanting him, for allowing himself to share physical contact with such a person, physical *pleasure*, for fuck's sake.

Mostly, though, Cal knew, the rage had been directed at Jewel, who'd taught him so well about racism and hate and fury – wanton fury, he guessed it was, and he thought that 'wanton' was a word he remembered from the Bible, and he'd liked it enough to include it once in his Epistle.

He hadn't planned any of it, though, neither the killing nor the destruction that had come after, but it had seemed to him at the time that he'd had no choice, that he just had to do it.

And then after the rage, after the *out*rage, once his rational mind had begun functioning again, he'd been surprised by how well he'd been able to go on thinking and planning.

But now the cops were out there looking for him – at least they were looking for someone, for an unknown *killer* – and he was shut away in this hole, and he knew he was going to have to be damned careful for a while, stay here for about as long as he could stand it, before he could risk going out again.

Being a joy-boy again.

12

His sister-in-law was in the kitchen when Sam came down in the morning.

Two-and-a-half hours' sleep before going back to work on a weekend morning – and that scrap of rest had been disturbed at around four thirty by Joshua's crying, though Sam had a fuzzy recollection of Grace waking instantly and saying she'd take care of him – but now his wife and son were still sleeping, which was good, and Sam had showered and shaved and was feeling at last half human, and he, like most of his colleagues, had been known to go to work on less rest than this.

'Aren't you a sight for sore eyes?' he said as he walked in and saw Claudia, in a black satin robe, standing watching the kettle reach boiling point.

'You, too,' she said.

Their hug was warm, their fondness real, though they'd seldom spent more than a matter of days together in the seven years or so that they'd known one another. But Claudia was Grace's beloved sister, which was all that mattered to Sam, and pulling back now to check her out, he saw what his wife had meant yesterday.

Strained was how she looked to him, and he'd like to have stayed home, caught up with her, spent time with his family, but there was a brutal killer to be caught and the usual stresses of his overdue paperwork mountain – and Sam had woken up worrying about Mildred Bleeker, even though he had given a cell phone to one of the night patrol guys to pass on to her. He and Martinez had agreed that it might be as well to put out a BOLO (police shorthand for 'be on the lookout for') on her silver stranger, and even though that man had probably had zilch to do with the killing, it was still troubling Sam that he might have seen Mildred watching him.

'Tea?' Claudia offered, aware of his antipathy to coffee.

'No, thanks.' Sam opened the refrigerator, took out the jug of squeezed orange juice, poured himself a glass and went to take Woody's leash from its hook, creating a wagfest and eager cries at floor level.

'I know you got in late,' Claudia said, pouring water on a teabag. 'I could take Woody for his walk, if it would help.'

'It would more than help.' Sam put the leash back, and the dog subsided in disappointment. 'You sure?'

'I'd enjoy it.'

He downed his juice, rinsed the glass, kissed the top of her head. 'Tonight,' he said, 'I promise we'll have some time.'

'Don't make promises you can't keep,' Claudia told him.

'I can promise to try,' Sam said.

It was comfortable, affluent suburbia. Lovely houses, lush palms, thick bladed lawns, colourful flowers and shrubs, well-maintained sidewalks.

The kind of road people could feel safe in.

Yet Claudia, changed into jeans, T-shirt and sneakers fifteen minutes later for Woody's walk, found she did not feel safe.

She'd had this feeling before.

Of being watched.

Not here, of course, but back on Bainbridge Island, all too recently, and on the mainland, too, on one occasion, in Seattle.

There she knew now that the feeling had been all too well-founded, but there was no one watching Claudia here, she knew that perfectly well, too, unless perhaps it was a neighbour taking a look out of their window at an unfamiliar dog walker; but still, it was unsettling enough to remind her of why she'd abandoned her husband and sons to come here.

She knew full well that she was going to have to tell Grace soon, not because her sister was inquisitive, but because she loved Claudia, and, of course, she was also a psychologist, accustomed therefore to picking her way over sensitive terrain until she struck emotional oil.

'OK, Woody,' she said to the dog. 'Time for me to face the music.'

Woody peed against a palm, and then he stood perfectly still, and growled.

'What?' Claudia said, the small hairs at the nape of her neck rising.

And then she saw the ginger tomcat, sitting on the path of a house just ahead of them, staring out Woody.

'Fool,' Claudia told herself, and went on walking.

13

No witnesses or leads as yet.

Nor a single clue as to where their John Doe had been slain.

No Missing Persons reports matching his description.

No instant miracles from the ME's office either.

Sam had received a text from Mildred a little while ago.

DEAR SAMUEL, THANK YOU FOR THE
PHONE. PLEASE DO NOT CONCERN YOUR-
SELF ABOUT ME. YOURS, MILDRED.

'She texts better than I do,' he said, showing it to Martinez.

'Maybe she had some help.'

'I wouldn't bet on it,' Sam said. 'Mildred's an enigma.'

'Doesn't mean her silver dude's our guy,' said Martinez.

'Means I'd like us to talk to him, though,' said Sam.

'You and me both,' said his partner.

14

'I had an affair,' Claudia told Grace, and then swiftly, desperately, added: 'Please don't hate me.'

Grace stared at her. 'I could never hate you. You know that.'

'I do,' Claudia agreed. 'But still.'

It was almost eleven, and they were in the den, a room often used by Grace in the past – and, she hoped, in the future – for seeing her young patients, its walls covered with their own brightly coloured paintings;

65

though for now it, too, had a playpen and a stack of soft toys – one of which Joshua, dressed in comfy blue and white rompers, was now contentedly snuggling up to after a fine game of 'find the rattle' with his Aunt Claudia.

'Do you want to tell me about it?' Grace asked.

She felt more than a little shocked, and mad at herself, too, for feeling that way, because as a psychologist, she knew she ought to know better. Except, of course, this was not a patient, this was her own sister, so she guessed she was entitled to feel a degree of shock, because Claudia had her sons to consider, and so far as Grace knew, with the possible exception that he might have railroaded his wife into relocating to Seattle, Daniel had always been a decent man, a good husband and father.

Things change, she reminded herself.

'It's all over,' Claudia said. 'It was almost before it began.'

It sounded crazily simple, as she told it. She had been at a very low ebb, low enough to be in a park on the island having a weep, when this man had stopped to ask if she needed help, and he was a stranger, but he was also kind and attractive.

'So you had an affair?' Grace could not conceal her amazement. 'On the basis of a

66

pick-up in a park?'

'Do you want me to tell you or not?' Claudia asked quietly. 'Because I'm finding this very hard, and I doubt that you could disapprove of me any more than I already do myself.'

'I'm not disapproving,' Grace said, knowing that wasn't entirely true. 'More surprised, I guess. And of course I want you to tell me.'

'There's not much more to tell,' Claudia said. 'It was very brief, but also very sweet. And, in some respects, good for me.'

'OK,' Grace said, and waited for her sister to go on.

'I'd been feeling so cold,' Claudia said, 'as if nothing could ever really warm me through again, and then suddenly there he was, and we had this *connection*, which I know sounds like a terrible cliché, but...'

'Go on,' Grace said after a moment.

'I knew right away – and I told him – that it was never going to be more than that, just those moments, nothing else.' Claudia shook her head. 'But truly, sis, he did make that cold go away for a little while, and though I guess he was using me, in a way, I was much guiltier of that than he was, and he knew that and he was OK with it, he was very kind to me about it.'

'Do you want to tell me his name?' Grace's first shock had given way now to a strange

67

kind of intrigue.

'Kevin,' Claudia said. 'He's from Australia.' She looked into her sister's blue eyes for an instant, found the even gaze too hard to cope with, looked away again. 'Do you mind if I don't tell you any more about him than that?'

Grace found that she did mind, because it seemed to emphasize the distance that had opened up between them over time. 'It's up to you how much you want to share.'

The door opened a little wider, and Woody came into the room and settled with a soft grunt of contentment on the rug beside the playpen.

'My guilt,' Claudia said. 'That's what I think I need to share most.'

'From my point of view,' Grace said, slowly, 'what I'd like you to feel able to share with me is why you were feeling so cold in the first place.'

'Loneliness,' Claudia said. 'Silly bitch that I am, with a good husband and two great kids, I still felt alone. Isolated, you know?'

'Sure,' Grace said. 'At least, I can imagine.'

And was, for about the millionth time, keenly aware of her own great good fortune.

15

Cal had emerged, relieved to be outside even if it was daytime, not *his* time, but beggars couldn't be choosers – which was not really true, it seemed to him, because panhandlers and street people seemed to have plenty of choice, seemed to have almost unlimited freedom in this great land, which was a damned sight more than he had right now.

Dangerous enough to be outside at all, but he needed food, and he'd bought a *Herald* and a bagel with cream cheese and a pint of Seagram's and a gallon of water and just a pint of milk because of the heat, and some apples and two Hershey bars and a big bag of Cheetos and some tall kitchen bags for trash. It was too goddamned hot for him, and he resented being forced to come out at this time because too much sun often made him feel nauseous.

Still, he'd decided he was going to take a little stroll along the beach, might as well now he was out, and it wasn't so bad, wandering over the sand like some aimless tourist, his sneakers dangling from one hand, his shopping in the other, but now he was moving past the piece of beach that he knew, from the Channel 7 News, was where the rowboat had been hauled ashore by the swimmer, and which he hoped to hell was still the closest the cops had to an actual crime scene.

There were plenty of people around, the rowboat long gone, of course, and all the tape too, and the cops. And Cal guessed he ought to feel relieved by that, by the reassuringly swift eradication of the human drama, yet instead he felt a pang of disappointment, as if he'd been cheated.

He'd expected a little more ... *something.*

No one so much as glancing his way, either, which was no real surprise since he guessed he looked like a regular guy walking on the beach today; no make-up, no gorgeous shimmer, and anyway, this was not his time, these people were not his kind, neither as playmates nor prey.

He spotted a pair of uniforms on the horizon, heading his way.

Cops.

Time to go back to the hole.

16

'How much does Dan know?' Grace asked.

'Nothing,' Claudia said.

'OK.' Grace's mind spun, trying to stay steady and, most of all, non-judgemental. 'But you're here.'

'Because I'm a coward.'

'No, you're not,' Grace said. 'Or you never have been.'

'It gets worse,' Claudia said.

Grace waited.

'I'm being blackmailed.'

'My God.' Now Grace was openly horrified.

Joshua was still in his playpen, occupied now with a soft ball. These past few disturbed nights aside, he was such a good, undemanding little boy, for whom Grace was as endlessly and passionately grateful as she was for Sam.

As she'd believed Claudia was for Daniel and their boys.

'Someone saw us in the park,' her sister went on, 'and took photographs. Of me kissing Kevin.'

'Who?' Grace's bewilderment was growing, because this kind of thing only happened to public figures or movie stars, not to suburban wives, and who would do such a thing to Claudia, or to Daniel, come to that?

'Still worse to come,' Claudia said, 'depending on your outlook.'

Grace waited.

'The blackmailer was Jerome Cooper.'

Grace stared, her mind floundering again. 'Roxanne's son?'

Claudia nodded, the flush in her cheeks darkening. 'Our stepbrother.'

Grace felt suddenly as if her thinking processes had been caught up in an internal mud storm, as if this was one ingredient too many, and certainly too bizarre. She never thought of Jerome Cooper as her stepbrother – she never thought about him at all, in truth.

Jerome Cooper. Son of Roxanne Cooper, who'd married their father back in 2000, two years after their mother's death.

She and Claudia had both felt relieved at the time not to receive invitations, had only found out about the marriage because someone (they'd never found out who, nor cared) had anonymously sent both sisters Xeroxes of the notice in the *Melrose Park Journal*, and of a wedding snap showing a middle-aged woman in a snug-fitting white suit – her only resemblance to their late mother her blonde hair, though that, Grace had felt uncharitably certain, looking at the photo, had come out of a bottle – standing between her new husband, Frank Lucca, and a grinning boy of about sixteen. After which there had been one combined Christmas and change of address card – the Luccas were still in Melrose Park, living in a street Grace thought was less than a mile from their old place – signed *Roxy, Frank and Jerome*, to which Claudia had reciprocated but Grace had not, and no communication since then.

More than seven years now since they'd seen Frank.

Grace, for one, had no regrets on that score.

'How,' she asked now, 'could Jerome possibly know about you and this man?'

Since to the best of her knowledge, Frank Lucca's stepson still lived just outside Chicago, over two thousand miles from Seattle.

'He must have been following me.' Claudia paused. 'He'd come to Bainbridge Island before.'

'He had?'

'He showed up on our doorstep out of nowhere last fall, looking for a hand-out.' Claudia shook her head, remembering. '"I'm Jerry," he said, "Roxy's boy." He has this really insincere smile.'

'You never said a word to me.' Grace was stunned.

'It was right after I'd come back from visiting with you guys.' Claudia had flown down after Joshua's birth and stayed on for a while to help. 'You'd all been through so much, and I didn't want to burden you.'

'And later?' Grace said. 'Why not tell me then?'

She looked down into the playpen, experiencing a strong urge to pick up her son, but Joshua was perfectly content, and her sister's need for her full attention was decidedly greater for the moment, so Grace remained on the sofa.

'Because I knew it would make you mad,' Claudia answered. 'And I guess I wanted to put it out of my mind. Dan saw how upset I was, and said that if the guy was in a jam, we might as well give him five hundred dollars, since he was, in a sense, family, but he asked Jerome to sign a receipt, and he didn't argue, said he was grateful and it'd be all he'd ever ask for.'

'Why did he say he needed this money?' Grace asked.

'He said his mom and Frank were going through a bad time.' Claudia paused. 'He said he figured *we* owed him. You and I.'

'How did he figure that?' Grace asked, harshly.

'The implication was, Daniel and I took it, that if we'd been better daughters and not run out on him and Mama, Papa might not

74

have had to close down the store and sell the old house when he married Roxanne, and things would have been easier ever after.'

'And we could have stayed home and sliced salami.' The bitterness was still in her tone, and Grace had never known till now, nor cared, if the Lucca's house move had been up or downscale. 'We could have made it easier on our father because we *owed* him so much.'

17

Sam and Martinez had been in the office screening all the reports called in to the whole Miami-Dade area that might possibly relate to the killing – the time frame now estimated by Elliot Sanders as having been between midnight and four a.m. Friday, give or take.

There had been a bunch of calls complaining about disturbances of the peace, but only two worth following up: both reporting awful screaming, both callers feeling that the screamers had sounded male. One in the Hallandale area, the other in Coconut Grove.

'If the killer set the rowboat adrift near the

crime scene' – Sam had been checking stats on currents and wind and tidal flow – 'then the Grove's a better bet for getting washed up on South Beach.'

'Coulda killed the guy up in Hallandale,' Martinez said, 'then found himself the row-boat further south.'

'Lot of driving around with the body,' Sam said.

'Or sailing around,' Martinez added.

All conjecture, for now.

But they took the Grove first.

Which led them nowhere.

Hallandale likewise.

18

'He came to the house last Monday morning while Dan was out, showed me a photo of me with Kevin, and told me he wanted ten thousand dollars. I told him the photo wasn't of me, told him to get lost.' Claudia reached down into her shoulder bag, pulled out a white envelope and withdrew a photo-graph. 'But even if it isn't the greatest shot, of course it's me.'

She held it out, her hand shaking.

'Are you sure you want me to look?' Grace asked.

'Of course I don't want you to look,' Claudia said. 'I don't want any of it to have happened, but I'm here because I need your help, so I guess you'd better see just how low and dumb your sister can be.'

Grace took the photograph, saw a couple in what seemed a tender embrace, thought of Daniel, a tall, angular man with kind, green, myopic eyes, who stooped a little from years of hunching over drawing boards and plans, but was still attractive and had always, Grace believed, been kind, and then forcibly pushed away that image.

'I guess,' she said, 'you could say it wasn't you.'

'Maybe,' Claudia said. 'If it was the only one.'

'Go on,' Grace said, dreading what was still to come.

'Jerome said he had plenty more photos, and any fool could see they were of me, and if he were me he'd think about this real hard, because it seemed to him I had a whole lot to lose, but because we were "family" he'd give me some time to think it over, but if I didn't come through with the cash, I'd be real sorry.'

'And then what happened?'

'He left,' Claudia said. 'And I've spent the past five days going out of my mind, waiting for him to come back, one moment making up my mind to tell Dan and pray he'll forgive me, the next telling myself that would be the selfish thing to do, because it might make me feel better, but not him, and of course I know that's hogwash, but...'

'You've heard nothing more from Jerome?' Grace asked.

'That was the other thing I kept telling myself: that Jerome had changed his mind, realized it wasn't going to be the easy money he hoped for, that maybe I would tell Dan and maybe even call the cops.'

'So why did you leave?' Grace asked. 'How could you risk leaving when Jerome might turn up again any day?'

'I couldn't face it,' Claudia said. 'I couldn't face Dan.' Her brown eyes sparkled with sudden tears. 'I couldn't go on lying every minute I was with him.'

'So what did you tell him about going away?'

'I told him that you were still having a bad time with baby blues, and I wanted to come see you, help out for a while.'

For the first time, Grace felt real anger at her sister. 'I'm over that, Claudia, and you know it, and I imagine you've told Daniel as much. I'm on the verge of starting to see patients again.'

'I had to tell him something,' Claudia said. 'I'm sorry.'

Grace saw despair in her eyes, and her anger dissipated. 'I still don't see how you can risk Jerome showing up when you're not even there. I don't get it, sis.'

'Me neither,' Claudia said, wretchedly. 'But then, I don't really get what happened in the first place, with Kevin.'

'I'm not sure that's quite true,' Grace said. 'You said you were at a low ebb, said you'd been feeling "cold", said—'

'Please,' Claudia said, quickly, 'don't be scornful. I don't think I can cope with that.'

'How do you think Daniel's going to cope,' Grace said quietly, 'if he sees the photos? When he realizes you lied to him about coming here, that you were escaping, running away.'

'You make it sound as if I want to hurt him.'

'I don't mean to,' Grace said. 'I know it's not in your nature to want to hurt anyone, and certainly not someone you love as much as Daniel.' She paused. 'That's assuming you do still love him.'

'Oh, God, yes,' Claudia said. 'That's why I left, don't you see? If I'd stayed, I'd have had no choice but to tell him the whole truth, and I couldn't bear the thought of seeing his face when I told him – and sure, I know it won't be any better if he hears it from that *snake*, it'll be even worse, but at least I won't be there.' She shrugged. 'I told you I'm a coward. Now you know.'

Joshua began, suddenly, to cry, and Grace

stood up swiftly to retrieve him from the playpen, Woody wagging his tail as she came close, then settling down again, resigned to being ignored.

'I guess I've been hoping,' Claudia went on, 'that maybe Jerome won't go to Daniel, because after all, what would be the point? Once Dan knows the truth, there's no hope of a payout.'

The baby had already stopped crying, but Grace, grateful for the comfort of his warm, solid body in her arms, began to walk back and forth in the small room, kissing the top of his head, consoled by him.

'So what now?' She stopped moving, looked down at her sister.

'I don't know,' Claudia said.

'Do you think,' Grace asked, slowly, already repelled by the idea, 'that I should call Frank?'

'God, no,' Claudia said. 'What for?'

'Intervention, maybe?' Grace said.

'Surely he's the last person in the world we want to talk to,' Claudia said. 'And I don't think for a single minute that he'd be interested in helping.'

'I guess not,' Grace said. 'What about Roxanne? Maybe if she knew what her son had been up to...'

'That would mean telling her what I've done,' Claudia said, appalled.

'Maybe she already knows,' Grace said,

then shook her head. 'I guess it's not my best idea.' She paused. 'Let's wait and see what Sam thinks.'

'Do we have to tell Sam?'

'Yes,' Grace said. 'It's the reason you've come to us.' She saw fresh misery in her sister's expression. 'I mean, I know it's your personal business, but now you've shared it with me ... I don't keep anything from Sam these days.'

'All right,' Claudia said.

'You said that you need my help, sis.' Grace sat down on the sofa again, settled Joshua on her lap, gave him his rattle. 'I'm just not sure – other than being here for you – what I can actually do to help.'

'I don't know that either.' Claudia paused. 'Maybe I just need you to help me work out why this has happened. Why I've done such destructive things, why I even looked at Kevin in the first place.'

Joshua was content again, sucking on his rattle, leaning into his mother.

Every last trace of Grace's exasperation had melted away.

'Have you really been so terribly unhappy?' she asked.

'Yes,' Claudia said. 'I rather think I have.'

19

The explosion sent the boat, in a thousand or more flaming fragments, soaring into the inky sky, then descending gracefully, like glowing snowflakes, back down on to the ruffled black waters.

People within a half mile or so experienced the blast as a near-physical shock, but the reverberation rolled further through Miami Beach and parts of Miami itself, waking and alarming some residents and visitors, startling birds and animals, sending humans reaching for their remote controls.

Sitting in the nursery rocking chair at four a.m. on Sunday morning, already awake because her son had begun crying twenty minutes earlier, Grace had been using the peaceful minutes since Joshua had quietened to float an idle hypothesis about the reasons she and Claudia had both become island dwellers of a kind, wondering if it might involve some sort of subconscious moat fixation, perhaps a lingering craving for protection from the bête-noire of their mutual past...

The boom of the explosion arrested the musing, started Woody barking and the baby wailing again.

'What the hell was that?' Claudia appeared in the doorway in cream satin pyjamas, not a hint of sleepiness in her face.

'Everyone OK?' Sam was there now, shorts just dragged on, Woody trotting in behind him, already over the noise and pleased now to find everyone awake.

'We're fine,' Grace said. 'It's all right, Joshua, sweetheart.'

'It sounded so close,' Claudia said.

'Probably not as close as it sounded.' Sam came into the room, crouched down by the rocker, kissed Grace's cheek and stroked their son's hair. 'It's OK, sweet boy, everything's fine.'

Joshua's crying was starting to thin again, more of a fretful, weary need for sleep now, his eyes round and anxious, and Grace handed him up to Sam, because it was not uncommon for his dad to be the one to hush him more swiftly, and sometimes Sam crooned softly to him in the fine baritone that had won him lead roles in S-BOP – the South Beach Opera – and Joshua plainly adored his daddy's voice.

'You think it was a bomb?' Claudia asked.

'Probably a gas explosion,' Sam said.

Grace glanced at him, had a sense that he didn't really believe that, but like him she said nothing more, perhaps choosing ignorance, at least for a while, because they had a baby son now who they longed to bring up in safety, and bombings of any kind as close as this spelled unacceptable horror.

'Magic touch,' Claudia said, looking at Joshua, already drifting off in his father's arms. 'Our two were always like that with Daniel.'

'I remember.' Grace saw the sadness in her sister's eyes, felt for her.

Sam lowered the baby carefully into his crib and settled his favourite small stuffed toy bear close by. 'Cup of tea, anyone?'

'So long as it's chamomile,' Grace said.

Claudia pulled a face. 'Hate the stuff. I'm going to turn on the news.'

'Why don't you try going back to sleep?' Grace suggested.

'After that?' Claudia said. 'No way.'

20

Cal was huddled naked on his thin, lumpy mattress, eating Cheetos, trying not to make crumbs, and watching the small black and white TV on the floor that his jackass-scumbag 'landlord' had seemed to think turned the shithole into a positive dump-de-luxe.

Hearing people saying that a boat had exploded, and watching the news crawls at the bottom of the screen confirming that much, was making him more nervous than the weird sound that had dragged him out of his shallow sleep, or even the small shock, two hours before that, of his cell phone ringing with its sharp, bird-like trill – Jewel having decided to pick tonight to call him after weeks of silence.

Witch.

'Don't imagine you can come back when you choose,' she'd told him, 'after all this time pissing around.'

Like he was yearning for her.

The early TV reports – still being generated mostly by residents, all jumpy as popcorn but milking their big news-maker moments – had been shifting the possible location and cause of the explosion back and forth. One minute, it was a bomb at Miami Beach Marina, next it was a gas cylinder explosion on a sailboat in Biscayne Bay, then an accident involving illegal immigrants on the Miami River, then a terrorist attack on a cruise ship in the port.

Cal enjoyed a good shiver of speculation same as the next guy, but all he really wanted right now was a chance to check out *Baby*, make sure she was whole, and for Christ's sake, he was paying good money he could ill afford to keep her safe and legally docked, which still seemed to him the best way to keep from attracting any interest from Customs or cops or even thieves. Not that she was exactly the style of cruiser anyone was going to be standing in line to steal.

If *Baby* had been blown to kingdom come, at least that would be one whole set of potential crime scene problems pulverized along with her.

He reached for his notepad and pencil, made a note of that word – *pulverized* – for the Epistle.

Nice word.

He'd felt it when the boat went up – and that was the one and only thing the news people seemed sure about, that it had been a boat, so someone had to know where, stood to reason. He'd been sleeping, so perhaps it had been part of a dream, but he thought that the shitty old window frames in his room had rattled, that even the cruddy bed, with him lying on it, had shuddered, which had made him think, seconds later, of sex.

Not a bad feeling at all.

Probably not so good if you were *inside* the explosion.

Or maybe that could be the best possible way to go.

Not yet though.

Right now, Cal wanted two things. To go see *Baby* and to start going out again, at the right time, the best time of night, seeing his kind of people again. Doing his thing, maybe making some money.

What he could use, financially, was another trick like the Wilmington woman, someone of means, preferably someone who'd stay *alive* after they'd paid him, so he didn't have to go through all that hassle and angst again.

Angst was another good word.

One he was familiar with.

21

In the house on the island, the phone rang at four-fifty, after Sam had come in off the deck where he'd been standing with Woody, listening to not-too-distant sirens, trying to pinpoint the location, wondering which of the TV reports was going to turn out to be right, knowing that he could have either made a call or simply listened to the police dispatcher to find out more, but actually glad, for now, not to be directly involved.

Grace and Claudia were at the kitchen table when the ringing began, had been about ready to go back to their beds.

'A bomb then,' Grace said as Sam came in to pick up the phone.

Nothing more than that occurring to her, no fears, just a general grim certainty.

'Oh my,' Claudia said, thinking of her boys.

'A fucking boat blew up,' Martinez was telling Sam. 'Alvarez wants us all in.'

'Where?' Sam asked.

'Biscayne Bay, south-east of Treasure Island.'

Too damned close.

'You picking me up?' Sam asked.

'In fifteen,' Martinez said.

Sam pondered as he dressed for work – suit, holster, Glock, the usual, since this early Sunday shift would be followed by a full day's work and maybe more – what exactly they might be up against here. It was too soon for anyone to know the cause of the explosion, unless there had been confirmed intelligence or perhaps a coded threat, in which case Homeland Security would be calling the shots, and then at the very least the FBI's Miami Field Office would be ruling the roost, with the ATF not far behind.

'Isn't this a job for the Coast Guard?' Grace asked, handing him a tie.

Sam nodded. 'Along with the Fire Department.'

'So why are you being called in?'

'I don't know yet,' Sam said, heading

88

out of the bedroom and back downstairs. 'If this is no accident, it doesn't automatically mean it's terrorism. Could be an old-fashioned kind of crime.'

'Lovely,' Grace said, right behind him.

'Or maybe this is just Alvarez or the Captain figuring that if someone's bombing Miami, people are going to get a little crazy.'

Grace kissed him at the door. 'Whichever, please be careful.'

'Always,' Sam said.

She wished, with all her might, that were true.

'What?' Daniel sounded bleary, as well he might at this early hour.

'I had to call,' Claudia said, up in Cathy's bedroom, 'because of the bomb.'

'What bomb?' Instantly awake. 'Where? Are you OK?'

'I'm fine.' She felt comforted hearing his voice, even more consoled because he sounded concerned, and because clearly there had been no visit from Jerome, at least not yet. 'I'm sorry to wake you, Dan, but we're all so wide awake here, and I just had to hear your voice.'

'What bomb, Claudia?' Daniel persisted. 'I don't know anything.'

She told him what little she knew. 'It must be something big for Sam to get called out like this.'

'That's what happens with cops, surely,' he said.

Plainly hoping to go back to sleep.

'I'm sorry,' Claudia said. 'I guess it was a shock. It made me want to check that my husband and children are OK.'

'We're thousands of miles away,' Daniel said, 'so of course we're OK.'

'Well, good,' she said.

She felt her hackles rising, wanted him to have said more, to have been happier to talk to her, whatever the hour, but then she reminded herself that their separation was entirely her fault.

Except Daniel didn't know that, and he hadn't even asked after Grace.

'Go back to sleep,' she said. 'And tell the boys I love them.'

'How's Grace doing?' he asked.

Guilt sent her spirit crumbling again.

'A little better,' she said.

'That's great,' he said. 'So when do you think you'll be coming home?'

'I'm not sure,' Claudia said. 'Soon as I can.'

'Right,' Daniel said. 'So if it's OK with you, I'm going to try and get a little more shut-eye before I have to get up and start our day for real.'

'Of course it's OK,' Claudia said. 'I really am sorry.'

'No problem,' Daniel said, and hung up.

22

It was still too soon to say what had caused the explosion, but first light had turned up, in the flotsam in Biscayne Bay, the destroyed boat's decal bearing its registration number. A Sunseeker 75 yacht, the most modest of a small fleet of yachts belonging to one Adrian Leehy, a big cheese music business guy with a part-time home on La Gorce Island.

Leehy and his family were all safe and sound in New York City. The yacht – named *Darryl* for Mrs Leehy – had apparently been stolen from its mooring sometime between eleven p.m. Saturday night, when the housekeeper had last laid eyes on it before retiring, and around three thirty, half an hour before the explosion.

No eyewitnesses to the theft, and though it had occurred on this island of immense wealth and private guard-gated security consciousness, it was too soon to say if the crime had been recorded on any surveillance system.

Three reasons had been given for the rousing of all available personnel in Violent

Crimes. One: the location of the explosion. Two: Adrian Leehy was not only wealthy, but he was also, according to Mike Alvarez, a hugely generous supporter of a cerebral palsy charity close to Chief Hernandez's heart. Both the police chief and the billion-aire happening to have a child with that disease in common, along with an apparent-ly great mutual respect.

There was a further, far more significant reason for the summoning of all detectives.

Something else had been found in the wreckage.

Human remains.

Claudia wanted to go shopping.

'I need some good old retail therapy with my sister and nephew.'

They had rested since Sam had gone to work, and now they knew as much and as little as the rest of the local population; namely that the explosion had occurred on a single boat, and so, because these things were known to happen accidentally now and then, it was unsettling, but so long as no one was hurt, life could perfectly easily go on.

And Grace and Sam did happen to have a glitzy mall practically on their doorstep, and suddenly an hour or two spent browsing through Neiman Marcus and Saks, and win-dow ogling Jimmy Choos and Tiffany jewels seemed just what Claudia needed.

'We can pop Joshua in his stroller and walk,' she said.

'It'll be much too hot for that by the time we're ready to come back,' Grace said.

The doorbell rang.

'Expecting anyone?' Claudia asked.

Grace shook her head and went to open the door, Woody glued to her heels, his sharp barking resonating in her head.

'Don't open it,' Claudia said.

Too late.

'Yes?' Grace said to the man on the door-step.

He was young, mid-twenties, with brown hair, a thin, weak mouth and beady light brown eyes.

'I don't believe this,' Claudia said from the hallway.

'I'm Jerome Cooper,' he said to Grace. 'Your stepbrother.'

'What the hell do you want?' Claudia came up close behind her sister.

Woody stopped barking and growled.

'I don't like dogs,' said Jerome Cooper.

'I do,' said Grace.

'Aren't you going to invite me in?' her stepbrother asked.

Grace didn't budge. 'What can I do for you, Jerome?'

'Shut the door, Grace,' Claudia said.

'You don't want to shut the door on family,' Jerome said.

'You're not family,' Claudia said, still right behind Grace.

'Claudia, go and call Sam,' Grace told her.

'Just shut the *door*,' Claudia said.

'Go ahead,' Jerome Cooper said peaceably. 'I won't push my way in.' When he smiled, his mouth stretched and became even thinner, but the eyes stayed sharp. 'But I won't go away either.'

'Claudia, make that call,' Grace said. 'Now.'

She shut the door.

Sam had gunned his Saab all the way up Collins, but there was no sign of Cooper by the time he reached the West Island.

A patrol car could have reached them five times over, but Grace had insisted that she wanted no official police involvement because they were in no danger, Cooper had made no threats, and patrol officers would mean reports, which neither she nor Claudia wanted.

'He just said he wouldn't go away,' Grace said now.

'But he did go,' Claudia said.

'Seems that way,' Sam agreed.

He had made several circuits of the small Bay Harbor Island community, but short of checking every garage and back yard and, to be certain, every room of every house in the district, he knew better than to feel wholly

94

confident that the creep really had departed.

'So what's going on?' he asked.

Grace had told him only half of Claudia's tale last night when he'd come in late from work; not because she intended keeping this from him, but simply because she'd figured that in the circumstances, hearing what a member of her father's new family had done, or tried to do, up in Seattle, was something that could easily wait.

Now the two sisters – with the baby perched on Grace's knees – sat in the kitchen, filling Sam in on the rest.

'OK.' Sam turned his attention square on Claudia. 'You've spent more time than Grace with this guy. Do you feel he could be dangerous?'

'No way,' Claudia said. 'He was mean, obviously – it was a mean thing to do, to say the least – but I never felt threatened, not in any physical sense.' She looked at Grace. 'Don't you think I'm right about that?'

'He has sneaky eyes,' Grace said.

A thought occurred to Claudia, causing instant, fresh distress. 'I hope you guys don't think I knew he might follow me here?'

'Of course we don't,' Grace said.

'It never entered my head, or—'

'Claudia, honey,' Sam said, 'we're not blaming you for this. I just need to know what this guy wants.'

'Presumably,' Grace said, 'what he wanted

before.'

'Money.' Claudia's eyes filled with tears. 'I'm so sorry.'

'It's all right.' Grace stood up and put an arm around her sister's shoulders.

'I need to know a little more,' Sam said. 'Anything you can tell me.'

'He's a scumbag,' Grace said.

'I should go home,' Claudia said. 'I should not have left.'

'You're not going home till you're good and ready.' Sam got up, went to the refrigerator, took out a jug of orange juice and offered it to the women, who both shook their heads. 'And definitely not because this blackmailing creep showed up here.'

'He didn't actually try that again,' Claudia said.

'Only because we didn't let him in,' Grace said.

'He'll be back.' Sam drank a glass of juice and checked his watch.

'You have to go,' Grace said.

'Alvarez knows I'm here, so I have some time.'

Life had become a little easier in the department ever since Sergeant Kovac, one of the banes of Sam's and Martinez's working life, had transferred out of Violent Crimes to Strategic Investigations and been replaced by Mike Alvarez, who was definitely one of the good guys. With no progress to speak of in the rowboat homicide, however, and the Leehy case fresh in their laps, Sam didn't want to push his luck.

'I'm going to ask a patrol to swing by a couple of times as a personal favour – no reports filed, don't worry.' He saw the sisters glance at each other. 'I'm not happy about leaving you here at all,' he added. 'So take it or leave it.'

'We were going to go shopping,' Grace said.

'Just over to Bal Harbour,' Claudia added.

Grace saw his hesitation. 'After all these years, Sam, I'm not prepared to let Frank make me a prisoner in my own home.'

'This isn't about your father,' Sam said.

'In a way, it is,' Grace said. 'By extension.'

'OK.' Sam gave in. 'But if you see him, just go sit somewhere real public and call me right away, and if he comes back here after you get back, do not open the door till I get here.'

'You can't keep shuttling back and forth,' Grace said.

'If some jerk plans on hassling my wife and sister-in-law,' Sam said grimly, 'you'll be surprised how often I can shuttle back.'

23

A second text from Mildred arrived a little after noon.

> DEAR SAMUEL, JUST TO LET YOU KNOW THAT I'M PERFECTLY FINE, THOUGH NIGHTS AROUND MIAMI DO SEEM TO BE JUMPING A LITTLE! YOURS, MILDRED.

Sam texted her straight back:

> DEAR MILDRED, THANKS FOR THE RE-ASSURANCE. I'LL HOPE TO COME BY SOMETIME SOON, BUT MEANTIME IF YOU NEED ME, JUST CALL. YOURS, SAMUEL.

Confirmation was in that the explosion had been no innocent accident, though it might prove to be a case of a bomber blowing himself up prematurely. The feds were on the case, as anticipated, along with the ATF working in cooperation, for the time being, with Miami Beach.

Sam and Martinez had been given the go-ahead, by Alvarez and the chief, to concentrate on their own homicide.

Lord knew their John Doe deserved their full attention.

Still nothing to identify him either. All they knew about him was that his last meal had been of spicy fish with rice and vegetables, that he'd had anal intercourse not long before his death – with no injuries to indicate that it had been non-consensual – and that his sexual partner had used a condom.

Still no Missing Persons reports that might match him.

'If he just started a vacation,' Sam said bleakly, 'it could be a couple of weeks or more before anyone notices he hasn't gotten home.'

'If he's a loner, or no one gives a fuck,' Martinez said, 'it could take forever.'

Sam had been checking in with Grace regularly.

'You're much too busy to keep calling,' she told him after they'd returned from Bal Harbour. 'If we see Jerome again, I promise to tell you right away.'

In the past, she'd have felt no need to reassure him of that. But the anxieties she'd kept from him last year had done some damage to the soft core of their fine and infinitely precious relationship, and Grace knew that she would never take that kind of risk again.

'I ran Cooper through the system, and

99

came up with nothing,' Sam said, 'which is good, so far as it goes, but I'm still betting he'll be back.'

'Claudia's trying to believe otherwise,' Grace said.

'How's she holding up?'

'By buying presents and spending much too much money, especially on us.'

'You shouldn't have let her,' Sam said.

'I tried, believe me, but she was unstoppable,' Grace said. 'She bought Cathy a pair of beautiful red and white shoes with wedge heels and ribbons, and while I was in the restroom with Joshua, she went into Tiffany and bought him the most gorgeous elephant moneybox – our son has a Tiffany moneybox, can you believe it?'

'I'm not sure I want to.' Sam was dry.

'Then – wait for it – she got us a Tiffany crystal bow box. I almost got mad at her, but she looked as if she was going to cry, so I gave her a big hug instead, and then we had some coffee at the Santa Fe and wrote postcards to Daniel and the boys.'

'She buy gifts for them too?'

'Not today,' Grace said. 'She wants to go to Aventura, which I'll make sure she does, because I'd hate for her to go home emptyhanded.'

'Not to mention penniless,' Sam said. 'Has she called Daniel again?'

'Not that she's told me.'

'I hope,' Sam said, 'this doesn't all spin out of control.'

'Me too,' Grace said.

That was one of the things about running away to lick wounds, Grace had come to see over the years; because it meant being away from the very person or people you needed to mend fences with, it often lengthened, rather than shortened, the healing process.

Vicious circles everywhere.

Sam took fifteen minutes out that afternoon to visit with Mildred.

He found her less than a hundred yards from her bench, feeding stale breadcrumbs to a bunch of birds, her bags at her feet.

She smiled when she saw him. 'You didn't have to come, Samuel.'

'Can't say I liked the idea of you being out here alone last night,' he admitted. 'It must have been a little scary, even for you.'

'Takes more than a little bang to bounce this old heart around,' Mildred said. 'But I did hear on the grapevine that some poor soul was killed in the bay. Is that true, Detective?'

'I'm afraid so.'

Mildred scattered the remnants of her crumbs. 'And was it a bomb, as they're also saying?'

'I don't know the answer to that as yet, Mildred.'

'And if you did, you probably couldn't tell the likes of me.'

Sam smiled at her. 'So how have you been, apart from having your sleep disturbed?'

'I haven't seen my *angel* again,' Mildred said. 'If that's what you're asking.'

'You'd have told me if you had,' Sam said. 'I didn't come to ask about that.'

'I know you didn't.'

He hesitated before asking: 'Are you still happy out here, Mildred?'

A down to earth approach always best with her.

'As a clam,' Mildred said.

24

June 9

Early Monday morning, Cal was out again.

At the real time. Night time. *His* time.

No make-up, no *gorgeousness*, just himself, but at least he could breathe better than in daytime, check out the action, see if there were any more cops sniffing around 10th Street and the promenade than there had been on Saturday.

First thing he'd done was take a slow walk over to Alton Road and north to 16th Street

– then an even easier, nonchalant kind of a stroll all the way west to the end of the road, and there was Flamingo Marina, and there was his *Baby*, and even though everyone knew now that it had been some rich guy's yacht that had gotten blown up in Biscayne Bay, it was still good to see her safe and sound, and he wasn't going to risk boarding her yet, just went on strolling past like some insomniac tourist out stretching his legs; but she looked just the same as before, like nothing special to anyone in the world but him, and Cal guessed that was good news, though in a weird way it offended him a little, as if people ought to realize that *Baby* was special.

That *he* was special.

He was back on Ocean Drive now, out among his kind – though there weren't enough people around for his liking, Sunday nights into Monday mornings being quiet out of season, but still, it was kind of buzzing, and things seemed so normal, as if none of that excitement had ever happened, neither the yacht explosion nor even the dead man in the rowboat on the beach – and Cal wished he could have been there himself to see that show. And if only he could take a risk on just *shimmering* himself up and turning a trick, he'd feel so much better, because boredom was making him hungry, and sexual frustration had always sharpened his appetite for food, and the garbage he was having to eat was unhealthy and fattening, and if he didn't get a decent fuck soon, he was going to end up with a goddamned paunch, which would just about kill him...

Oh, but it was still so good just to be out in the warm, humid darkness, hearing the music and good-time voices, with the late birds flitting around, some of them exotic, some just plain tawdry, all full of their own needs but all the more human for that. And Cal suddenly felt such a powerful connection to them all that he had a great urge to rush up to a whole *group* of them, to grab one and embrace them, hold them close and risk whatever came next, a punch or a kiss on the mouth or even a knee in the groin.

But he knew he couldn't get too close to anyone, knew he needed to stay penned up inside himself for now, a stunning bird suffocating under the drab camouflage of a Joe Blow. And it was hard, knowing that in a while most of these people would melt away into the night, and then it would be just the stragglers and a few of the hard core left; those who, like him, lived to be out here at this hour, and the others, who had no real choice.

He wasn't sure if he'd been looking for *her*, the stinky old bird, but he saw her just the same, all bundled up in her layers, slumped on the bench near the kids' play area like so much wrapped up human trash. Yet despite his instinct to recoil from her, he found he just could not resist walking right by her as a kind of test, though even if she'd been staring right at him the other night, he doubted if she'd have recognized him now, because it was so much more than cosmetics and clothes that set him apart, it was the fact that Cal couldn't walk his walk tonight, couldn't offer up joy to anyone.

There was nothing from her. No reaction at all.

Which was insulting in one way, but more good news in another, because it confirmed to him that he was a true chameleon; that if he were to walk three feet from a cop, he would not get noticed, which meant that he could probably take someone right *now* if he chose to, could seduce them right off the sidewalk or grass or sand and take them somewhere like the dunes and fuck them or even strangle the life out of them, and no one would notice until they fell over the corpse.

But it wasn't supposed to be *that* he was hungry for. It was supposed to be carnal pursuits – though maybe there was nothing much more carnal than what he'd done to the last man he'd fucked, than what he'd done to his flesh...

He realized he'd grown hard just thinking about it.

Took a swift glance down at his pants, checking that it didn't show, and it did not, which was, in a way, a great waste.

Cal sighed.

No cops around, which was good news too, so maybe soon – maybe even tomorrow or the next night – he could be himself again.

Joy-boy.

Joy-giver.

Mildred had seen him.

At least she *thought* she had, but she had not been, still was not, sure.

He'd smelled different as well as looking it, had been moving completely differently, but then, just before he'd disappeared from sight, she thought she'd detected a small jauntiness to his walk.

'Just a tiny little giveaway,' she said to Donny, her late fiancé, to whom she still spoke regularly, day and night.

Yet even if she'd wanted to, she still could not have described him to Detective Becket, because what she'd recognized in him was something so indefinable. Besides which, it was dark and he was wearing a baseball cap and the kind of clothes that ten million or more men wore every day, and she'd had to take great care not to stare at him, because she had felt him looking at her, had felt that he'd walked past her to test her reaction, which was why Mildred had made out that she was fast asleep, had not moved so much as a wrinkle.

No silver shimmer about him tonight.

No angel.

But still she'd felt it about him.

Death.

25

Finally, a Missing Persons report that sounded as if it might be their John Doe.

Sanjiv Adani, a twenty-four-year-old receptionist at the Hotel Montreal up near Collins Park, AWOL from work since Friday, and no one at the hotel had apparently been concerned enough to consider filing a police report; but then he'd missed his mother's birthday party yesterday evening, and when his family had failed to reach him by phone, they'd known something was very wrong.

'The brother says he'd never miss her birthday,' Martinez told Sam.

The man in the photo faxed along with the report had his arm around an older lady, probably his mom, and he had smiled at the camera. He was good-looking, slim and, judging by the lady's expression, she loved him a lot.

'Family events are a big deal in Adani's life,' Martinez went on. 'Mom and Pop live in Surfside; older brother, Barun, the guy who made the report, lives in Aventura. Their younger sister, Anjika – all three kids single, by the way – lives in New York City, but she came down for the birthday.' He checked his notes. 'Adani has a one-bed on Bay Road near the Lincoln Road Mall. A colleague at the hotel, woman name of Gloria Garcia, says he used to share his apartment with his Cuban boyfriend.'

'Used to,' Sam echoed.

'They broke up about a month back,' Martinez said. 'Ms Garcia says she never knew the boyfriend's name.'

Sam looked back at the photograph.

Remembered the state of their John Doe.

Looked again at the woman they were presuming to be Sanjiv's mother.

Had the grim certainty they were about to break her heart.

The other two men of the family – father Bhupal and older brother Barun – came to the Miami-Dade Medical Examiner's office behind Jackson Memorial Hospital to make the identification.

From photographs, which was intended to make the ordeal a little easier, though nothing in a case like this was going to make anything remotely better, and Sam was never certain in any case if seeing photos of a loved one's face, wounded or not, but appearing somehow disembodied because of the wrapping around the head, might not sometimes be even more terrible for the newly bereaved than seeing the body itself.

No doubt from either of these patently anguished men that the deceased was Sanjiv Adani.

'I didn't want our dad to come,' Barun, a tall, handsome man in dark suit and tie, told Sam and Martinez after his father had left the Family Grieving Room to go to the restroom, insistent on going alone, 'but he wouldn't hear of anything else, said it was "*dharma*".'

'What does that mean?' Martinez asked.

'It has many meanings,' Barun said, 'but I guess "duty" pretty much covers it today.' He wiped his eyes. 'A father's duty.'

They waited in silence until Bhupal Adani emerged from the restroom looking haggard and haunted.

'I apologize,' he said.

'No need, sir,' Sam said, and was glad to see Barun take his father's arm.

Sam and Martinez had both seen shock and grief more times than they could remember, but it never got easier for either of them.

'I looked up Sanjiv's name on one of those websites,' Martinez told Sam later, as they got back into his Chevy Impala. 'It means "living".'

'I did the same,' said Sam. 'My definition was "reviving".'

'Seemed like nice people,' Martinez said.

Neither of them was in any hurry to meet Sanjiv's mother.

26

Mildred sent another text, enjoying this new small skill.

Shades and tiny glints from another time. Another life.

ALL IS WELL OUT HERE, SAMUEL. BE SAFE. YOURS, MILDRED.

She had decided, after all, against mentioning last night's passer-by.

It had probably just been an old woman being fanciful in the dead of night, and nothing, in any case, that could help the police – and the last thing Mildred Bleeker wanted was to become some foolish attention-seeker.

'Not my style,' she said to Donny.

And Detective Samuel Becket had more than enough to concern him.

27

The Adani house, on Carlyle Avenue in Surfside, had a red-tiled roof and peach-coloured shutters at the windows, and looked a compact, well-cared for home.

The grief in the atmosphere inside felt thick enough to slice.

Barun, who'd let the detectives in, showed them into the living room and introduced them to his parents. Sanjula Adani, dressed in a white sari, was seated beside her husband on an emerald green couch in the centre of an old-fashioned room with photographs and small Indian watercolours on the walls, and two small, but glistening chandeliers overhead. The bearing of both parents was erect and dignified, yet they seemed scarcely present, their minds, Sam and Martinez both realized, in dark and terrible places.

'I've just made some tea for my parents.' Anjika, their daughter, wearing a white T-shirt and jeans, came in with a tray. 'Would you like some?'

'Anji,' Barun said, rebuke in his tone.

His sister rolled her reddened eyes in irritation, then explained: 'My brother's reminding me that Hindus in mourning aren't supposed to offer food or drink to guests.'

'It's all right,' her father told her. 'Go ahead, Anjika.'

'There's no need,' said Sam.

'Nothing for me, thank you,' Martinez said.

Barun beckoned them back out into the hallway. 'If you can, gentlemen,' he said softly, 'I'd be very grateful if you could put your questions to me.'

'If we can,' Sam said, 'we will.'

They moved into the kitchen, a room that looked and smelled well used, the air redolent with spices, and Barun invited them to sit at the white-clothed table.

'As I'm sure you can imagine, it's all proving too much for our mother,' he said. 'And our father...' His voice faltered, then strengthened again. 'Sanjiv was gay, which I'm only mentioning in case it has any relevance for your investigation. But our father's always been in denial about that, so if you were to ask him questions about my brother's lifestyle, he wouldn't exactly lie to you, but you still might not get the whole truth, you know?'

'We understand,' Sam said. 'Thank you for telling us.'

'Do you think your brother's "lifestyle" is

relevant, sir?' Martinez asked.

'I have no idea,' Barun Adani said, 'but you read about such things.'

'Yes, sir,' Sam said. 'You do.'

'It's different with our mom,' Barun continued. 'She's only ever wanted us all to be happy and safe, though I know it upset her that Sanjiv might never give her grandchildren – and I think she was always afraid for him, too.' He shook his head. 'Not of anything like this, though. Never.'

Sam watched his composure crack, saw the well-mannered young man struggling not to fall apart, bowed by the pressure to hold it together on his family's behalf, and felt for him, imagined future years loading on to his shoulders, how much those bereft parents would need him, not just to comfort them but to fulfil their dreams too.

Anjika came into the kitchen, a cell phone to one ear, listening mostly, answering in monosyllables. New York perhaps already tugging on her, Sam surmised, then guessed too that however much she loved her family, she'd probably be back there as soon as she decently could, and who could blame her?

'I'm sorry.' Barun was back under control.

'Don't apologize,' Sam said. 'Just a few questions.'

'Of course. Anything I can do.'

Anjika, still on the phone, slipped back out into the hallway.

'You said you hadn't seen Sanjiv for two weeks,' Sam said. 'How was he then?'

'He seemed fine. Well, and quite happy.'

'Have you spoken to him since?' Martinez asked.

Barun nodded. 'Three, maybe four times. We talked regularly.'

'Do you know if anything unusual was going on in his life, or if he had any special plans?' asked Sam. 'Did he share his private or business news with you?'

'Sometimes.' Barun shook his head. 'I've been trying to remember anything that might be useful, but our conversations were usually snatched. We caught up with each other, nothing much more.'

'So he didn't mention,' Martinez said, 'where he was going, or who he was planning to see, on Wednesday or Thursday?'

The last twenty-four hours of a homicide victim's life being generally considered the most important period by the investigators, right along with the first forty-eight hours after the discovery of the body.

'No, sir,' Barun said.

Too much missing time in this case.

'We heard,' Sam said, 'that your brother had a boyfriend.'

'He did, but they broke up a while ago. Eddie Lopéz.' A quirk of Barun's mouth betrayed a touch of disapproval. 'A dancer. I only met him once. Sanjiv told me he'd been in *Cats* and some off-Broadway shows, but so long as they were seeing each other, Eddie was just a nightclub dancer.'

'We heard they were living together,' Martinez said.

'That's right, for about three months.' Barun had lowered his voice again. 'But they were never right for each other, and I think Sanjiv knew it, even if he never said so.'

'Do you know who broke it off?' Sam asked.

'Eddie walked out on my brother.'

'Did they fight, do you know?' Martinez asked.

'If they did, Sanjiv didn't tell me. My brother was a hard worker. He wanted to move up the ladder, dreamed of opening his own boutique hotel someday.' Barun's dark eyes were sadder than ever. 'He was a romantic. He once told me he liked having someone to take care of, and I think he used to cook for Eddie, even clean for him.' He paused. 'Sanjiv did once say that when he got home too dog-tired to do anything, Eddie didn't like it much.'

'So was it a volatile relationship, would you say?' asked Sam.

'Not that I know of,' Barun said.

'How did Sanjiv seem after López left him?' Martinez asked.

'Unhappy,' Barun said. 'But then he seemed to pull himself together, said he was going to concentrate even harder on work. My brother had a lot of drive.'

Anjika, off the phone at last, came back into the kitchen, laid a hand on her brother's shoulder in a brief gesture of warmth, then turned without a word and went back to their parents in the living room.

'Did Sanjiv and your father fight about his lifestyle?' Martinez asked.

Barun shifted in his seat. 'Is that relevant, Detective?'

'Probably not,' Sam said.

Barun sighed. 'Sure they fought sometimes. Dad wanted him to be a lawyer or a doctor – or at the very least, a rather disappointing accountant like me.'

'And how did it go,' Sam asked, 'when Sanjiv chose hotels?'

'Our dad does disappointment very well. I mean, he knows how to show it.' He gave a small, wry smile. 'Even better than our mom, and I'm sure you know something about Indian mothers.'

'I had a Jewish mother,' Sam said.

That often threw people off for a moment, but Adani was too immersed in his loss for more than the mildest curiosity. 'Then you'll know,' he said.

'Do you know where we could find Eddie López?' asked Martinez.

'I don't have a clue,' Barun said.

'You could try Satin,' Anjika said, coming

quietly back into the kitchen. 'It's a club in Calle Ocho.'

Barun Adani frowned. 'How would you know that?'

'Sanjiv told me,' his sister answered simply.

'Were he and Lopéz still in touch?' Barun asked.

'Our brother was lonely,' Anjika said.

And her eyes began to brim.

28

David Becket had invited Grace and Claudia to lunch.

'I know I shouldn't,' Claudia said in her sister's Toyota, looking back over her shoulder at Joshua, buckled into his seat in the rear, 'but I feel kind of apprehensive seeing Saul these days.'

'I can't imagine why,' Grace said. 'He's fine, and he loves what he's doing.'

'Woodwork instead of studying medicine?' Claudia turned her face to the window, stared out at the seemingly endless string of lavish apartment buildings and hotels and the ocean beyond, sparkling blue in the sunshine.

'Saul makes furniture,' Grace said crisply.

'He has a real talent for it which he discovered long before he got injured, and he *chose* to change direction, it wasn't just foisted on him – and I'm not at all sure that it doesn't suit him more than medicine might have.'

'Still living with his dad, though.'

Grace shot her a sideways glance. 'I hope you're not planning on taking this negative attitude to lunch.'

'I'm just telling you how I feel,' Claudia said. 'Or have I lost that right too?'

Grace slowed the car a little. Traffic on this section of Collins was even lighter than usual today, which meant they were going to be there in no time, and she wanted to get past this before they reached the Golden Beach house.

'What are you talking about, sis?' she said. 'What rights have you lost?'

Claudia's hands clenched into fists in her lap. 'I've strayed,' she said, tautly. 'I've committed adultery. I've been a total fool. I've abandoned my sons and left my husband to fend for himself without so much as an explanation.' Her eyes filled. 'I've lost the right to be *me*.'

Grace saw a turning up ahead into a small hotel car park, glanced in the rear-view mirror, then swung in and stopped the car.

'Come here.' She put out her arms, and Claudia leaned against her and began to weep. 'You've lost no such rights at all,' she told her. 'You've been human, that's all. Don't cry, baby.'

'But what I've done to Dan is so terrible.'

'You've done it to yourself too,' Grace said. 'And I know you'll find the way to put it right again, if that's what you want to do.'

'By telling him, you mean,' Claudia said desolately. 'But what if he can't forgive me?'

'I think he will,' Grace said. 'Because I'm guessing that he loves you way too much to want to lose your marriage.'

'So long as I don't wait too long.' Claudia pulled away.

'You're going to have to judge that for yourself, sis.'

Only one of many judgement calls that Claudia was going to have to make, Grace supposed. And no sign of Jerome Cooper since yesterday morning, but still...

'Are you really up to this lunch?' she asked.

Joshua, who'd been awake but content until now, who was in general an excellent traveller, gave a sudden squawk of impatience.

'It's OK, sweetheart,' Grace told him. 'We'll be on the move again in a minute.'

'We don't need a minute,' Claudia said. 'I'm OK.' She opened her purse, found a tissue and wiped at her eyes. 'I'll be fine.' She looked back at her nephew and smiled. 'It'll do me good to focus on someone else for a change, won't it, Joshua?'

And Joshua beamed at his aunt, sealing the deal.

'Let's go visit with family,' Claudia said.

29

Sanjiv Adani's home was no crime scene. Anjika, having given Sam and Martinez nothing further to work with, their subsequent search, warrant obtained, of her late brother's apartment – a second floor walk-up in a two-storey house on Bay Road, a few blocks from the Lincoln Road Mall – provided little more in the way of clues.

The essentially intrusive task of sifting through the remains of a dead person's life had never come easily to Sam. When the victim was as tidy as Sanjiv Adani, the job could be at least more swiftly accomplished, but the results, all too often, tended to be nothing more than skin deep. No tell-tale stains, no unwashed crockery to provide prints or DNA, no old garbage to sift through, no give-away, or at least, intriguing Post-it stickers on the refrigerator door.

Adani had been a neat, hygienic man and also, on the face of it, a conventional one, his home showing the influences, the detectives felt, of both his upbringing and his good hotel training.

'There's order and quality here,' Sam said. 'Not just show.'

'How does falling for a male nightclub dancer sit with that?' asked Martinez.

'Maybe he just fell in love,' Sam said.

'Let's don't forget lust,' Martinez said.

The photographs on display in Adani's sitting room were all of family, but his bedside table drawer yielded a black-and-white publicity shot of a bare-chested, well-muscled but lean and darkly handsome young man, signed in thick blue pen: *For Sanjiv, from your crazy boy, Eddie.*

'He kept it after the break-up,' Martinez said. 'So I guess maybe love.'

'Or infatuation,' Sam added.

They found nothing in the apartment to indicate a wild lifestyle. Tylenol and an old, unfinished bottle of Valium were the only pills in the bathroom cabinet, alongside a couple of decongestant nasal sprays and a collection of colognes, body balms and antiperspirants. An old Dominick Dunne novel with a scarlet leather bookmark thirty-two pages in, sat beside the bed, which was neatly made with clean blue linen, nice quality pillows and no bedspread. A black linen shirt, laundered and pressed, lay on the top sheet.

'A reject, maybe,' Sam conjectured, 'while

he was getting ready for his last night out.'

'Sharp,' Martinez said.

'Maybe not as sharp as what he actually wore,' Sam said.

They found no hints of where he might have been heading on Thursday evening. Nothing on his computer – which they would, of course, still take away for more detailed inspection – no journal, nothing marked on his *New Yorker Cats* calendar.

'Not even his mom's birthday,' Martinez pointed out.

'He might not have needed to mark that down to remember it,' Sam said. 'Or maybe he keeps another calendar at the hotel some-place we didn't get to see.'

They already knew that Adani had no office or even a personal drawer at the Mon-treal; only a steel locker, in which they'd found a clean pair of Y-fronts, a pressed white cotton shirt, a wine-coloured tie with the hotel's M motif embroidered on it and a book about the Ritz Hotel in Paris.

'Is this all a little antiseptic?' asked Mar-tinez now. 'Kind of dull?'

'Maybe,' said Sam, taking another look around the sitting room. 'Or maybe it's just like we figured: he was a good, well-trained son.' He paused. 'With dreams of his own.'

'And a horny dancer ex-boyfriend,' Mar-tinez added.

★ ★ ★

Eddie Lopéz had a rap sheet. Minor stuff, mostly – reckless driving, felony possession and prostitution misdemeanors.

'And one arrest for domestic battery,' Sam noted, back at the office.

Which sent Lopéz to the top of their list of one, but with Satin – the Little Havana nightclub mentioned by Anjika Adani – not set to open till evening and no one there responding either to the doorbell or their phone calls; and with too many Eddie, Eduardo and Edward Lopéz listings in Miami-Dade to start trawling through until they had no choice, Sam and Martinez decided to head back over to the Hotel Montreal instead.

It was a nice enough place, a three-star hotel, superficially well-run and maintained; a fair bet for a young man planning an upward learning curve in the business. The manager, Carl Lundquist, had only good things to say about Adani, but Gloria Garcia was still the most loquacious and, at least on the face of it, the most caring that her colleague had been murdered. Though neither she nor anyone else on duty had anything immediately helpful to offer the detectives.

No quarrels between Adani and other personnel that anyone was willing to talk about; no run-ins with hotel guests; no promotion over another colleague that might have left a sour taste. No complaints or even grumbles

123

against the dead man. No love affairs originating in the hotel. No one knowing that much about Adani, described by two people as 'private'.

They wrote down names, addresses and telephone numbers, took lists of off-duty personnel, of shift and agency workers, copies of the recent guest register and duty rosters for the last two months; anything that might help them to assemble as full a picture as possible of the victim's working life.

On the way out, they passed Gloria Garcia in reception.

'I just remembered something,' she said.

'Please,' Sam said, hope rising, 'go ahead.'

'I remembered the boyfriend's name was Eddie,' she said.

'Nothing else?' Martinez said.

'I know it isn't much,' she said.

'Anything you remember is a big help,' Sam said.

And hoped she hadn't seen the exasperation in his partner's eyes.

30

David Becket, grey-haired, hawk-nosed, even more rumpled-looking these days than he had been prior to his semi-retirement, had always possessed a wonderful knack with people. With children especially, making him – his medical skills aside – such a popular paediatrician, and with the adult patients, too, who'd flocked to the free walk-in downtown clinic he'd run with a colleague for a number of years. He had fine, sensitive instincts, usually knowing when to push troubled people and when to leave them in peace. Which was a gift Grace liked to think she shared, but which she'd also had to learn to set aside on occasions as a psychologist with less than an hour at a time to draw her patients out.

Saul had it, too, this gift of warmth.

'Hey,' he said, coming out onto the driveway as they arrived. 'All my favourite people.' And then he swept his baby nephew up in his arms, and Joshua squealed with pleasure.

'Almost all,' David added.

'Sam sends you both big hugs,' Grace said.

'Cops,' Claudia said. 'Always working.'

And then she flushed, remembering Saul's lost love, who had also been a cop.

'Don't be so sensitive,' Saul said, easily. 'I'm not.'

His voice was still huskier than it had been, a legacy of last year's horrors along with the scars on his neck and some residual stiffness in his right shoulder, but Saul was alive and well and content with his ever-growing ability to create beautiful and useful items out of fine wood.

'It worries me sometimes,' David had said to Grace a month ago, 'that he's never going to get properly back out there while he's working and living with his old man.'

'He gets out,' Grace had told him. 'And I have absolutely no doubt that he'll leave when he's good and ready. You worry too much.'

Now, David looked across his living room at Saul, sitting on the floor with Joshua's aunt and the baby, all playing with fabric bricks and a big stuffed dog.

'What's up with Claudia?' he asked quietly.

'She has a few problems,' Grace said.

'I'm sorry to hear that,' David said. 'Anything I can do?'

'I don't think so,' Grace said. 'I think she'll be OK.'

And wished for that to be true.

31

Sam and Martinez were at Satin a half-hour before opening.

'Lopéz quit.' The manager, Manuel Vega, was tall and bald, his open-necked shirt wet with perspiration, feeling impatient and not troubling to conceal it.

'When did he quit?' Martinez asked.

Vega shrugged. 'A few days ago.'

'We need a date, sir,' Sam said.

'It's about a week ago.' The manager mopped his face with a checked handkerchief, then stuffed it back in his pants pocket. 'You need details, it'll take some time.'

'About a week' meant before the killing.

Not what they'd hoped for.

'We need them,' Martinez said, anyway, glad to piss the guy off.

'Why did Mr Lopéz leave?' Sam asked.

'Like I said, he quit, I didn't fire him.'

'Didn't he give you a reason?' Sam persevered.

'Dancers like Lopéz are a dime a dozen.' Vega shrugged again. 'He didn't tell me zip, I didn't ask.'

'He get a pink slip?' Martinez wanted to know.

'Sure,' the other man said. 'Everything legal here.'

'Glad to hear it,' Martinez said.

'I don't want any trouble.' Grudging respect shown for the first time.

'We're not here to give you any, sir,' Sam said. 'But we would appreciate any information you can give us on Mr Lopéz.'

'I can find you the address he gave us,' Vega offered.

Sam thanked him, then asked if Lopéz had been friendly with any of the other dancers or staff at the bar.

'Go ask them.' Vega pulled out his handkerchief again, mopped his glistening forehead. 'I gotta take a shower before we open up.'

'We'll ask them OK,' Martinez said. 'Right now we're asking you.'

Manuel Vega glowered at him, then turned to Sam. 'I don't recall him being special pals with anyone, but I mind my own business. So long as the dancers dance and the bartenders pour drinks, we all get along.'

'You haven't asked,' Martinez said, 'why we're interested in Mr Lopéz.'

'Like I told you,' Vega said, 'just another dancer.'

'Yeah,' Sam said. 'A dime a dozen. You told us.'

★ ★ ★

They were getting nowhere.

No one at Satin had anything helpful they were willing to share, not even the slightest hint of subtext or innuendo. Lopéz, they all said, had been easy enough to get along with, but had kept himself to himself.

'Private,' Sam remarked between interviews. 'Like Adani.'

'Not a hanging offence,' said Martinez.

And so it had gone on, no one giving them anything, except for one waitress, a pretty young woman called Trina, who thought he'd been in a relationship, but if he'd ever mentioned the other guy's name, she could not remember it.

'But he said it was a guy?' Martinez said.

Trina shrugged. 'He didn't need to.'

No joy at Lopéz's apartment either, a third floor walk-up two blocks from the club. No answer at his front door, his mailbox on the first floor unlocked and overflowing with junk mail and bills, and none of the dancer's neighbours responding to their knocking either.

Their luck changed for a few minutes as they were leaving, when a man came from the rear of the house taking out two bags of trash. In his early forties with a neatly trimmed beard and deep suntan, he seemed relaxed about stopping to speak to them, set down his bags and took a close look at their badges, then told them that his name was John Houlihan and that he 'kinda' remembered a guy living in 3D.

'Gay guy, yeah?' he said, his voice a little hoarse, then shrugged as neither detective responded. 'Close-shaven, earrings – one or two, I can't recall – but he was real slim, in great shape, couple of tattoos on his arms. Sound like your man?'

'Just like him,' Martinez said.

'I wish everyone was as observant,' Sam said.

'I never really talked to him though,' Houlihan said.

'When did you last see him?' Sam asked.

'I'm not sure.'

'In the last week?' asked Martinez.

'Maybe.' Houlihan's precision seemed to have departed.

'Any chance you could be a little more specific?' Sam said.

'Not really,' he said, then gave it some more thought. 'Maybe Thursday or Friday.'

Sam and Martinez both waited, their silence pressing him to go further.

'I guess Thursday,' he said, then shook his head. 'Tell you the truth, I've been a little out of it the last few days. I'd be a darned liar if I told you anything else.'

'That's OK,' Sam said easily. 'You wouldn't happen to remember what Mr Lopéz was wearing when you saw him on Thursday?'

Remembering Mildred Bleeker's slim 'silver' guy and hoping for a break.

Houlihan stroked his beard. 'Maybe jeans and a black tee?' He shook his head again and picked up the trash bags. 'I can't really be sure, I'm sorry. That could have been some other time.'

They noted his name and address and thanked him for his cooperation, then got back in the Chevy and headed back to the office to issue another BOLO and write up their report to date.

Looking for two men now in the Adani case – maybe the same man, though more probably not, they both thought. Neither of whom they had any grounds at all to list as suspects.

Getting nowhere.

32

June 10

The doorbell chimed at six ten on Tuesday morning, while Grace, Claudia and Joshua were still sleeping and Sam was in the shower, waking up.

Woody, therefore, the only one to hear the

131

bell and rouse the household.

Grace was still pulling on her robe as she peered through the upstairs hall window and saw Jerome Cooper on the path below, smiling up at her with his thin smile, wearing a short-sleeved white shirt and navy trousers and looking like a salesman.

He waved at her.

'Great,' said Grace as Claudia emerged from Cathy's room and Woody raced back and forth, up and down the stairs, still barking. 'Woody, be quiet.'

'It's him, isn't it?' Claudia said.

'What's happening?' Sam came out of the bedroom, a maroon towel draped around his waist.

'Jerome's back,' Grace said.

'Oh, God,' said Claudia, and began to cry.

'It's OK,' Sam told her. 'You don't have to worry.'

He went back into the bedroom, came out again ten seconds later in grey T-shirt, track pants and sneakers, and went downstairs, his body language resolute as hell, Woody glued to his heels.

'Oh, *God*,' Claudia said again.

'Sam, be careful,' Grace called, then turned to her sister. 'Stay with the baby while I get some clothes on.'

'But Sam might—'

'Sam and I can handle Jerome,' said Grace.

★ ★ ★

132

'Hi, Sam,' the man outside said, and put out his hand. 'I'm Jerry Cooper.'

Sam took the hand just so he could assess the grip. He'd known limper, but the other man's skin was clammy and his eyes were sneaky, just as Grace had described them.

'You'd better come in,' he said.

Like the handshake, that went against all Sam's instincts, asking a blackmailer into his house, but this was his wife's stepbrother, and needs must.

Jerome Cooper looked down at Woody, who was growling softly.

'Don't mind him,' Sam said.

'You sure?' Cooper asked.

'You're welcome to leave,' Sam told him. 'Your choice.'

'I know it's kind of early,' Cooper said, 'but I wanted to make sure of finding you home.'

'You succeeded,' Sam said. 'You coming in or not?'

'Sure.' Cooper flicked Sam a swift look of dislike, then checked out the small dog again.

'It's OK, boy.'

Sam stepped back to let the visitor in, and Woody skittered deeper into the house, wavering near the kitchen door while his master debated where to conduct the confrontation. The kitchen felt too private, likewise the den, which was also where Grace often saw her young patients, which to Sam's way of

133

thinking made it even more off-limits to known scumbags.

'In there's fine.' Grace, coming downstairs in jeans and T-shirt, nodded towards the den, making the decision for him.

'We could stay right here in the hall,' Sam said.

'I don't see why we shouldn't be comfortable,' Grace said.

She went ahead into the small room and sat down on the couch, Woody trotting in right after her and settling by her feet while Sam remained standing; and this was one of those times, he decided, when it felt real good to be five or six inches taller and a whole lot more powerful than a bad guy.

'So...' He didn't offer him a seat, found the man's presence an affront to the innocence of the children's paintings on the walls, noticed that for the first time this cosy room felt too small. 'What do you want, Cooper?'

'Jerome,' the other man corrected. 'My friends call me Jerry.'

Sam's eyes hardened, but he said nothing.

'At least this time I guess I got asked in,' said Cooper.

'My husband asked you a question,' Grace said, glad of her own composure, even if it was superficial. Not that there was any fear in her, not with Sam in charge, but she was, she found, filled with anger.

'So formal.' Cooper lifted a mousy eyebrow. 'Mind if I sit?'

He took a step towards the couch, and Woody growled again.

'Not there,' Sam said. 'The armchair.'

Cooper sat, then looked at Grace. 'How much has Claudia told you?'

'That you tried to blackmail her,' Grace said.

'Which is a felony,' Sam said. 'For which a person can be jailed, in case you're unclear about that, Mr Cooper.'

'Please.' Jerome's voice turned a little whiney. 'We're family.'

'For the last time,' Sam said, 'what do you want?'

'Money.' Cooper shrugged. 'Same as last time.'

'And same as last time,' Sam said, 'you can forget it.'

'Isn't Claudia coming down to say hi?' Cooper asked Grace. 'Only it doesn't feel right – it doesn't seem *nice* – having this little talk without her.'

'Five minutes.' Sam checked his watch. 'Then you're out of here.'

'The photographs,' Cooper said.

No more smiling, all pretence gone.

'My sister-in-law already told you to get lost about the photographs,' said Sam.

'They're amazingly clear pictures,' Cooper said, 'of my *stepsister*' – he emphasized the word – 'with her boyfriend groping her titties and his tongue down her—'

'Enough.' Anger resonated in Sam's deep voice.

'You bastard,' Claudia said from the doorway. 'You loathsome dirtbag.'

'Nice to see you, too, Claudia,' Cooper said from the armchair.

'I already told you.' Claudia had put on a tracksuit, feeling a need to cover up, and she was much too warm now but still trembling. 'You're not going to get a dime for your nasty little snaps.'

'Not so nasty,' Cooper said. 'Though I guess it depends on your viewpoint.' He paused. 'If your boys were to see them, for instance.'

'What do you mean?' Claudia's voice was shaky.

'My step-nephews, I guess you'd—'

In one motion, Sam had him out of the chair, one hand twisted around the fabric of his white shirt, the other gripping his left arm, and Grace was on her feet too, and Woody was up and barking again.

'Out, slimeball,' Sam said, propelling him past Claudia, out into the hallway and towards the front door.

'You let *go* of me,' Cooper protested.

'Sam, be careful,' Grace warned, because an assault allegation was the last thing he needed after last year's suspension.

Sam opened the door, steered Cooper

through it. 'You come within a mile of my family again,' he said, 'and I'll have you charged before you can blink your mean little stoat's eyes.'

'You want Robbie and Mike to see those photos?' Cooper stood his ground.

It came to Sam abruptly that maybe this man had a screw loose, because no one in his right mind would make these kinds of threats in front of a cop.

'Don't you even mention their names again!' Claudia flew suddenly past Sam, her eyes blazing with fury.

'Hey' – Sam let go of Cooper, grabbed her arm – 'take it easy.'

Upstairs, Joshua began to cry, and the small dog's barking grew more agitated.

'Claudia,' Grace called from the hall. 'Come back inside.'

'You go anywhere near my sons' – Claudia was shouting now – 'and I'll *kill* you, so help me!'

'Ten thousand bucks,' Cooper said, 'and you'll be rid of me for good.'

'Claudia, get inside,' Sam told Claudia.

'I'm not asking for a fucking million,' Cooper said, 'just ten lousy grand.'

Sane, after all, Sam decided as Claudia went back into the house, because they were out in public now, so if any of them laid a hand on him now it would be their word against Cooper's, and then the photographs would be on record, too, and Sam would have liked nothing more than to take this bastard into custody, but he wasn't going to play into his hands.

'You all owe me that much,' Jerome said.

Joshua was crying more loudly, and Grace badly wanted to go to him, but her own composure was long gone, and she wondered suddenly if maybe this was Frank playing a game with them...

'We owe you *nothing*,' she said, pitching her voice over the baby and the dog's barking.

'Both you sisters,' Jerome called right back, 'owe me big-time, and you' – he turned to Sam again – 'you can afford it, Mister Big Shot Detective living in your wife's fancy house on this nice little island.'

'What I can afford' – Sam took two strides closer – 'is to throw you in a real *nice* holding cell, with some real *nice* types.' He gripped Cooper's arm again, twisted him around. 'What I can *afford* is to kick your offensive little butt right off my property.'

'You're going to be so sorry.' Jerome's face was red-patched with fury.

'I don't think so.' And suddenly the need to kick the man's ass was too great to resist, so Sam did it, just hard enough to send Cooper sprawling. 'Now get the hell out of here.'

It took Jerome Cooper a moment or three to get himself off the grass, but when he was back on his feet, his eyes were meaner and harder and threatening.

'You are *so* going to wish you hadn't done that.'

'Not if I live to be a thousand,' Sam said, and went inside and shut the door.

'I'm sorry,' he said to Grace, who was at the top of the staircase, the baby in her arms, and to Claudia, now sitting on the second step up, pale and tearful. 'I couldn't help myself.'

'Of course you couldn't,' Claudia said. 'I'm glad you did it.'

Sam looked up at Grace.

'Me too,' she said, 'in a way.'

Sam felt the rage starting to melt away, leaving him shaken and a little sickened, and he always hated it when anger got the better of him, and it rarely happened, God knew, but that didn't make it right, and it certainly didn't make it wise.

'Know what you mean,' he said.

33

There had been another explosion.

Another yacht, this one in a marina up in Fort Lauderdale.

No connection with the Leehy family or corporation.

'FDLE reckon this one could be kids,' Mary Cutter was telling Riley as Sam came into the office. 'Same as last year.'

The Florida Department of Law Enforcement, originally created back in the late Sixties as the Bureau of Law Enforcement, provided services in partnership with local, state and federal criminal justice agencies to prevent, investigate and solve crimes while protecting Florida's citizens and visitors. There had been a similar boat-targeted problem up and down the Gulf Coast about a year earlier perpetrated by a group calling themselves the 'Bang Gang'.

'I thought Naples PD caught them all,' Riley said.

'Plenty more kids in the sea,' said Cutter.

'You OK, Sam?' Riley asked.

'Yeah, fine,' Sam said, trying to lighten up. Jerome Cooper on his mind.

34

Cal was finally back on board *Baby*.

Nothing ventured, he'd decided on waking that morning. And best to go in daylight, with plenty of people around, and if it turned out that the cops were waiting for him there, then so be it.

No one so far.

The little marina was quiet, no activity on or around any of the neighbouring boats, just a couple of guys and a middle-aged woman looking about ready to take out a well-maintained Chapparal cruiser over on the other side.

No cops.

Everything on board was just as he'd left it. Nice and shipshape on deck and in the cockpit.

Nothing overtly wrong down below either, unless, of course, you were *looking* for evidence of something having happened here.

Like sex and death.

The bike was OK – Daisy, his sexy tandem pick-up cycle – taking up too much space down below, and that had been one of the tough parts the other night, getting Daisy below instead of leaving her chained up on deck as he usually did, but he'd figured he couldn't afford for her to be visible, so he'd got the job done – and a whole lot more besides.

All visible traces of what had happened after that last seduction were gone, along with his Walmart comforter – and its blend of his-and-his DNA – and the old rug (a threadbare, smelly thing that had come with the cruiser) in which he'd wrapped up his *friend* until he'd been able to wash him down and roll him into the rowboat. The comforter and rug and the other man's clothes and wallet – out of which he'd stolen all of the sixty-five bucks that had been in there (which made him a thief, too, now, not like back in Wilmington), but none of the credit cards, because he wasn't a *fool* – and the gloves Cal had worn to protect his own hands, had all been taken out to sea, weighted down with some bits of broken slabs taken from a dumpster outside a building on 16th.

Gone.

Cal wasn't exactly sure why he hadn't sent the dead man the same way. Especially considering all the physical effort and emotional strain that had gone into stealing the damned rowboat, let alone making the transfer.

The closest guess he could pin down was that he was, at heart, an exhibitionist. That maybe he wanted what he'd done to be seen by someone.

Not that he wanted to be caught and put back in the slammer, Jesus, no.

But if no one ever found out what he'd done, how would anyone ever get to know what had been done to *him*, how he'd suffered? And just telling someone like a shrink about Jewel and stuff wouldn't be nearly enough, because all that would make him was just another guy in therapy, no one giving a damn about him.

Prison, though. Just the thought of it...

142

Not forgetting Death Row and Florida's lethal injections.

That made his soul cringe, OK.

Which meant that he should not have done that, should not have taken all those risks, should not have stolen that rowboat and rolled *him* in and waited to see what happened next.

Nothing had happened.

Not so far, anyway.

The stink of bleach was still there, had jetted right up his nostrils the instant he'd boarded *Baby* again, catching at the back of his throat and bringing it all vividly back.

What he'd done to him.

Not the cord around his neck, nor even the ending of his life.

What he'd done *after*.

At least the guy had already been dead, hadn't gotten to know what that felt like.

Cal knew about that.

All about it.

Work to be done.

He'd gone shopping on his way over from the pisshole, had brought more bleach with him, and a roll of plastic trash bags and new rubber gloves and a pack of surgical masks from the drugstore. And a new, cheap white quilt from a kitschy bargain store with some god-awful name like Good Nite, but the quilt would be soft enough for sleeping on

143

when he felt ready to come back for real.

He hadn't needed a new scrubbing brush, because the one he'd used was still here, stashed in the storage space between the cabin floor and the hull. And that was another curious decision he'd made, because every last damned *atom* of the head on that brush had to be coated with DNA, so he ought to have sent that down into the deep with the other stuff, but he hadn't wanted to, had chosen to keep it, though again, he couldn't say precisely why.

You do want to be caught.

Maybe.

You want to use it again.

Maybe that too.

35

Jerome Cooper didn't have a criminal record, but that didn't make Frank Lucca's pathetic, blackmailing stepson any less of a sleazeball, and just the thought of him coming near his family again was making Sam feel sick to his stomach.

'I spoke with a pal in Bay Harbor PD,' he told Grace on the phone. 'No big production, don't worry, no explanations, just letting them know we've had an unwelcome visitor, so they can keep an eye open.'

'Surely they wanted to know a little more than that?' Grace was dubious.

'I told them a half-truth, said it's a family thing, and they understood.'

He and Grace had formed a number of good relationships on the islands, though back in '98, before they'd begun living together, it had concerned Sam, for her and Cathy's sake, that some people might not be too keen on having a black homicide cop in their midst, even if he was moving in with a psychologist pillar of their community; but those issues had been laid swiftly to rest, as they'd made him welcome almost from the beginning.

He hoped now that their kind, well-mannered neighbours hadn't spotted him kicking Cooper's ass that morning.

Though maybe if they'd known a little more about the bastard, they might have applauded.

Which was more than Barun Adani – who'd telephoned earlier to request a meeting – was likely to do when he came in to the office this afternoon.

No progress on the investigation into his brother's homicide.

That was sickening, too.

36

'So now what do I do?' Claudia asked Grace at lunchtime.

She'd been hiding out in Cathy's room for most of the time since Cooper's visit, but Grace had finally come to get her a half-hour ago, and now they were at the kitchen table, Joshua between them in his highchair.

'Call Daniel, I guess,' Grace said. 'Tell him what's happened.'

'Over the phone?' Claudia was horrified. 'I can't do that to him.'

Grace waited until Joshua had swallowed down the previous spoonful of squash, then offered him the next. 'I'm not sure you really have too many choices.'

Claudia sat in silence, unable to eat the avocado salad she'd prepared for the two of them, because the imagined photographs were making her feel nauseous, and the thought of Robbie or Mike ever seeing them was enough to make her want to scream.

'If Jerome's given up on the money,' Grace went on, 'he may just want to upset the boys out of pure spite. You can't risk that happening without somehow warning Daniel.'

Claudia imagined Robbie at his computer, opening mail, seeing...

She gave a low, choking cry, pushed back her chair and ran from the kitchen.

'Baba,' Joshua said, picked up a soft bagel from his highchair tray and waved it at Grace. 'Baba nooga!'

'Absolutely right, sweet boy,' his mother said, her heart aching for her sister.

Such tough times ahead for her, no matter how she handled it from now on.

And not a damned thing Grace or Sam could do to help her.

'Are you OK?' Daniel asked, on the phone.

'I'm fine,' Claudia lied. 'Missing you all.'

She'd gone straight up to Cathy's room and made the call right away, but knew already that she could not bring herself to tell him.

Monstrous coward.

'Maybe you should just come straight home.' Daniel paused. 'Perhaps Grace would like to come visit with us for a change?'

'She has Joshua,' Claudia said. 'It's not that easy.'

'Moms travel with babies all the time,' Daniel pointed out. 'And if Sam can't take time out to come along, he's always struck me as a pretty self-sufficient guy.'

'I'll talk to them about it,' Claudia said.

'Will you?'

There was a touch of disbelief behind the words that chilled Claudia.

What if he *knew*?

If he knew, she told herself, he'd have come right out and said so.

At least said *something*.

The fact was he did not know anything, either about her infidelity, or about the photographs or blackmail.

'I miss you,' Daniel said. 'We all do.'

Pure shame flooded her. She opened her mouth to speak, to confess, just blurt it out, deliver the hammer blow to their marriage, and then she shut it again.

'Claudia?'

'I miss you too,' she said. 'But I think that if you don't mind coping just a little longer, I'd like to spend a few more days here. Try to do a little bonding with my nephew, as well as help out.'

'If that's what you'd like,' Daniel said, stiffly, 'I can cope.'

'Are the boys OK?' Claudia said. 'No problems?'

She wanted to tell him to find a way to make their computers crash, to shut down their email servers, have their home fax numbers suspended, make sure that he checked any regular mail that might come addressed to them.

Maybe, it occurred to her suddenly, she could persuade Daniel to bring Robbie and

Mike down to Florida, and for a moment brilliant hope flared – and then she remembered that in the first place, Daniel wouldn't leave his business or take the boys out of school so close to the summer break on their mother's whim.

And in the second place, Jerome was here.

Anyway, their mother was not only an adulteress, but a liar. Who might not even deserve to have her sons with her just yet.

'They're doing fine,' Daniel answered her question. 'They're good kids, you know that. They understand you wanting to be with your sister and Joshua.'

'Just a few more days,' Claudia said.

Maybe by then she'd find the courage to face him again, to tell him the truth. Try to start putting things back together.

Maybe Jerome Cooper would creep back home to Chicago, and none of them would ever hear from him again.

If only.

37

Barun Adani had come to police headquarters to ask the detectives if they could help him achieve the speediest possible release of his brother's body.

Sam found them an unoccupied office away from the bustle, a little less bleak, he hoped, than an interview room.

The subject matter bleak enough on its own.

'Do you know anything about Hindu beliefs with regard to death?' Barun came directly to the point as Martinez brought in three cups of coffee.

'Just a little,' Sam said, and looked at his partner. 'Al?'

'Even less,' said Martinez. 'I'm sorry.'

'We believe – or are meant to believe – in reincarnation,' Barun explained. 'In the soul passing at death from one body to the next.'

In ordinary circumstances, he went on, family members would pray around the departed as swiftly as possible, and traditionally the body was cremated within twenty-four hours of death.

'When people die suddenly, as with my brother...' His self-possession fragmented a little, and he looked down at his hands on his knees, took a moment, then continued. 'When the deceased has had no time to prepare for death, tradition has us abandon the full rites – I guess so as not to hold up rebirth.'

'Which all makes any official delay especially rough,' Sam said, 'but I can assure you that everyone concerned will be—'

'Yes, I know,' Barun cut in. 'Everyone's

doing their best, and I'm aware that ours is not the only faith where time is of the essence, but day by day it seems clearer to me that we all have to take care of our own.' He shook his head, embarrassed. 'I'm sorry to seem rude.'

'You're being honest,' Sam said.

'It's only that for our parents, being unable to do things the right way for Sanjiv is making the whole ordeal even more unbearable.'

'You need to try and make them understand–' Martinez leaned forward in his chair, his eyes sympathetic – 'that this isn't just about a bunch of red tape. It's about making sure nothing gets overlooked, not by the ME, not by us, so we can catch whoever did this to your brother.'

'But you could at least speak to them?' Barun persisted.

'Of course,' Sam said. 'No question.'

'We wanted to talk to you again anyway, sir.' Martinez shifted the emphasis of the conversation. 'To find out a little more about Sanjiv.'

'The more we learn, the better,' Sam said. 'About your brother's habits, about the places he liked going to, any pastimes or hobbies.'

'We need lists,' Martinez added, 'of his favourite restaurants and bars, maybe nightclubs, even stores he regularly visited.'

'Any friends you might have forgotten

about,' Sam said, 'or old pals he might have been corresponding with.'

'Anyone who might have harboured bad feelings about him,' Martinez said.

'Sanjiv had no enemies,' Barun said. 'I'm certain of that.'

'I'm sure you're probably right,' Sam said. 'But we're trying to paint a picture of your brother's life, which means the good things, the really ordinary details, can often be just as important.'

He liked the man, thought Martinez did too. Not that it mattered a damn if they liked the grieving relatives or not, but the truth was that maybe it sometimes did serve to strengthen their resolve just a little more.

Not doing enough for this guy or his family, that was for sure.

38

It was the first time since the homicide that Sam had made it home for dinner at a decent time.

Claudia, Grace told him, was upstairs lying down, had said she had a headache and no appetite. Joshua was sound asleep.

He had his wife all to himself.

'I've missed you, Gracie.' He leaned against

the wall close to where she was working, watched as she tossed a spinach salad, then reached quickly for her left hand, brought it up to his lips and kissed her fingers.

'Me too,' she said.

'So how's our son doing with all this atmosphere?' He kept his voice low.

'He's great,' Grace said. 'He loves his auntie, and she's very good around him, takes care not to let things show too much.'

'Claudia's a good mom,' Sam said.

'Two thousand miles from her own sons,' Grace said.

'Is that a reproach, or sympathy?'

'A little of both, maybe.'

The table was already laid, so Sam grabbed a corkscrew and opened the waiting bottle of Sangiovese, sniffed the cork and set the bottle down again to breathe. Being married to a fine cook with an Italian heritage had zero disadvantages, he'd long since decided, except that these days he found he needed to work out for longer to keep himself in halfway decent shape. Grace liked to keep their food healthy on the whole, but treats like the pumpkin ravioli, and spinach and cheese *agnolotti* that she brought in now and again from Laurenzo's on West Dixie were indecently fattening, and the workouts just got harder and harder as time went on.

No complaints. *Lord*, no.

Sam sliced ciabatta, brought the bread and

salad to the table, poured some wine, and Grace brought over the rest of the dinner and sat down with him, smiled as she saw his obvious pleasure, saw him starting to really relax, then served herself and began to eat. Her hair was still butter-gold, still felt like pure silk when Sam ran his fingers through it, which he never stopped wanting to do. It was cut a little shorter than it used to be these days, but was still long enough for her to tie back or pin up, and every hairstyle seemed to make a different statement, brought out a different aspect of her.

Sam loved them all.

Pinned up casually this evening, a few stray hairs escaping in wisps, stroking her neck. Sexy as hell.

'This is wonderful,' he said.

'Good.' She'd made *polpettone*, a Tuscan-style meatloaf she tended to prepare as comfort food. 'Though I made it partly for Claudia.'

Sam's mind went back to the unpleasantness, took a sip of wine. 'Are you still sure you don't want me to go after Cooper?'

'That's the problem, though, isn't it?' Grace said. 'His name may be Cooper, but he's also a Lucca.'

'Which means what?' Sam said. 'You can't want to protect that slime.'

'Certainly not,' Grace said. 'I just don't want anything to do with Frank. Neither of us does.'

'I know how you both feel,' Sam said. 'But if this does go on, if Cooper does come back, we may not have much choice.'

Grace picked up a forkful of meatloaf. 'Do you think he believes what he said about us owing him?' She put the fork back down, the food untouched. 'Does he honestly think it might have been easier for him and Roxanne if Claudia and I had stayed in Melrose Park?'

'I don't give a damn what he thinks,' Sam said, 'so long as we never have to hear from him again.' He ate for a moment, then wiped sauce off his plate with a piece of ciabatta. 'I have to say I'm not happy about leaving him out there.'

'Because he's a creep, or because you think you made him mad?'

Sam eyed Grace. 'You think I shouldn't have kicked his ass.'

'I think – I know – his ass needed kicking.' She paused. 'But a lot of creeps carry knives or guns.'

'I shouldn't have humiliated him,' Sam said.

She looked at him, her brow furrowed. 'Do you think he really might be dangerous?'

'I doubt it,' Sam said. 'But I think I'm going to be watching all our backs until we're sure he's left town.'

'I think,' Grace said, 'I'm not sorry to hear that.'

39

June 11

At ten past midnight on Wednesday morning, Cal was in the dump behind Collins, almost ready to go back out.

All silver again. Looking *good*.

He'd brought his stuff back from *Baby*, because he'd realized he just couldn't wait any longer to get out there. Brought his face paint and silver eye make-up and special clothes and shoes. And, of course, Daisy, which had maybe drawn a little more attention to himself than was wise as he'd turned into the alley and opened the door to his godforsaken pit.

Not nearly so much attention as he planned to attract a little later.

They didn't all care for bike-riding, but the fun ones did, the worthwhile ones.

So no more rotting away in this hole, waiting.

Cal the joy-giver was aching to walk his walk again.

First find the *one*.

Then ride away to *Baby*.

Share the joy.

He'd decided to go straight back to Menagerie on Washington, partly because it was one place that opened every night except Monday and was always jammed, but mostly because of the luck it had brought him the last time.

That thought jarred him, made him stop to wonder just what it said about him that he considered that chain of events *lucky*. And then he chose to stop wondering about it.

Life was all about choices, and whatever worked for you.

He'd never had as many opportunities to choose before.

Different now. He was different.

Growing more so every day.

Every night.

40

Sam couldn't get to sleep, which often happened in the early stages of a new case, and especially when progress was as frustratingly slow as on this one. Part of the problem being that cases stayed *new* for such a brief time – and they were already way past those critical first seventy-two hours after the discovery of the crime, which was bad news in itself.

They owed Sanjiv Adani more than this.

Grace was sound asleep, for which Sam was grateful, and Lord knew he was fond of Claudia, but he was worried that this whole thing was going to bring Grace down again just when she'd been getting back on track, and so he couldn't help but hope it might not be too long before her sister felt ready to go home.

He got up as silently as he could, pulled on shorts and a T-shirt, and headed for the nursery for a swift fix of Joshua Jude Becket.

Except his aunt had gotten there before him, was standing over his crib.

Sam stopped outside, not wanting to intrude, but Claudia had already seen him.

'Please,' she whispered. 'Don't mind me.'

He came inside, and for a few moments they both watched the small boy, deep in the sleep of perfect innocence, his soft baby mouth slightly open, both arms out to the sides, little hands palms up.

No fears yet in this sweet, trusting human. Even when strangers came to call or stopped to take a closer look at him out of doors, for the most part Joshua either just smiled or looked back at them with interest or, sometimes, open curiosity.

Watch over him, Sam prayed silently, as he did each night.

Claudia smiled at him, and he saw that her

eyes were wet.

He felt guilty for wanting her gone.

'Cup of tea?' he asked softly.

Claudia shook her head. 'I'm going to try and sleep now.'

'You OK?' Sam asked.

'Getting there,' she answered.

But looking at her, even in the dim light, Sam didn't really believe her.

41

Menagerie was heaving.

Bodies everywhere, thrashing to the pounding music, ninety per cent male, young, middle-aged and older, black, white and all shades in between. Good times.

Cal had been here for a while, and there was no shortage of meat around, that was for sure, but no one yet to light his fuse. He'd been drinking Taaka Dry, which was supposed to taste of juniper berries, though if he could, he'd be sipping a really great Tanqueray, but with the costs of keeping *Baby* safe, not to mention renting the scuzzy pit, *plus* no tricks, he guessed he was lucky he could still afford to buy any gin at all.

Besides, his luck was about to change, because there was a guy looking at him.

Really looking.

Not Cal's type at all, no *way*.

But there was something buzzing between them, something going *down*.

And if this dude had a wad to match the bulge in his pants...

Cal downed the rest of his Taaka, took a long, steamy look right into the guy's dark eyes, and then he turned and walked his *slow* walk, kept on going until he was out of the bar and in the lobby and through the door out into the night heat on the sidewalk.

And if that guy was not following him right now, being tugged along in the joy-giver's wake, then Cal would most certainly eat his proverbial hat.

Here he comes.

Wouldn't be *hat* he'd be eating.

42

Mildred Bleeker could not sleep.

It was one of those nights when she just couldn't seem to settle, and usually the mix of ocean and the constant thump of SoBe partying back on the Drive lulled her to rest, but once in a while she got what she could best describe as *spiky*. Not unrelated to what her mother used to call 'ants in her pants', but not exactly the same either.

Edgier than that.

And the only thing she could do when she got this way was to walk.

When she'd been younger, more vigorous and less unsightly, she'd swum in daylight hours, but as she'd grown older and more wrinkled she'd taken to swimming late at night, which might be against the law but was kinder on the eyes. These days, though, having become less spry, she walked instead, during the day and at night too.

Anyway, as content as Mildred was with her lot, she figured everyone needed a little change of scene now and again. So she window-shopped like other people and, towards the end of opening hours, she picked up little snacks from her regulars, most of them spread out along Washington Avenue all the way from 7th to 11th Streets. Lord knew those leftover tacos and sandwiches were better off inside her than in a garbage can, and on occasions Mildred liked running errands for those good people who trusted her to mail their letters or even make deliveries for them, and there was nothing like a little mutual respect to make the world go round. Though some people's faces when they saw her coming in, say, to the dry cleaners with one of her regular's dresses or suits, could be a picture, but that didn't offend Mildred, no, sir, it just tickled her.

She didn't do trash cans, ever.

'Never ever,' she'd promised Donny a long time ago, one night on the street when she'd imagined he was watching and distraught and maybe even mad at her for sinking so low.

She had done soup kitchens when she'd had no choice; same with hurricane shelters, but she'd only slept in a homeless shelter once, and as kind as those people had been, it had just about killed her foolish pride, and that was one of the reasons she stayed around Miami Beach, because at least, she reasoned, it wouldn't be the cold that finally got her.

Lord, she hated the cold, always had.

Planting her feet one after the other on the stony sidewalk this night, she hoped she wouldn't have to walk too far before she got tired enough to go back to her bench and sleep, because her calluses were extra painful and her knees weren't what they had been either.

Then again, nothing much was.

43

'Call me Tabby,' the guy had said, out on the sidewalk.

A weird beginning, Cal thought, though maybe there was a little something *kitty* about the way the man moved, all dark brown in his silk-looking shirt and slinky-tight pants and pricey looking leather belt, and he remembered seeing a cat one time with chocolate-coloured fur kind of like this guy's.

Good Lord, Jewel would spit poison if she could see him now.

'I'm Cal,' he'd said, then elaborated: 'Short for Caligula.'

The other man's smile had been amused. 'I like that,' he'd said. 'But just so you know, I'm not interested in paying.'

They were still outside Menagerie, customers walking in and out.

Cal had been silent for a moment, disappointed, and a little pissed off too, because this guy could *afford* to pay.

'No offence,' Tabby had added, 'but I don't need to pay for what you can give me.'

'You'd be surprised,' Cal had said, 'what I

can give you.'

'Works both ways,' said the other man. 'Believe me.'

The glint in his black eyes had hit Cal's groin hard, and suddenly he'd known he didn't give a damn about the money.

'Take my arm?' he'd invited.

'Don't mind if I do,' Tabby had said.

They were strolling now, sauntering along Washington, first past Mansion (closed to-night, which was fine by Cal, because he hated the types who stood in line and put up with bouncers picking and choosing who got through the doors and then paid through their stupid spoiled noses to drink with a zillion tourists) and then passing across from the great white cop shop on the corner of 11th, and they weren't all that far now from his pit – not that they were going *there*, no sirree – and it gave Cal something of a buzz knowing his hideout was practically under the cops' noses. Still, that was one of the reasons he'd chained up the tandem three whole blocks from Menagerie: too close to the club might have maybe been like leaving some kind of calling card, in case someone had noticed it the other night, and too near the police station was just *asking* for trouble.

'So where are we going?' the stranger asked.

He smelled of something Cal believed

164

might be jasmine, and though he had no gift for identifying perfumes, he knew what he liked, and that nice scent seemed like a bonus, so he paused for a moment and kissed Tabby on the mouth, and found that he tasted of Jack Daniel's, which Cal had never liked, but then again, he'd tasted a whole lot worse on the mouths of strangers.

'We're going to my boat.' Cal started walking again. 'If that's OK with you.'

'You have a boat?' Tabby smiled and tucked his arm a little more snugly through Cal's.

'A small cruiser,' Cal said. 'Nothing fancy, but all mine.'

'Boats make me horny,' Tabby said.

And Cal realized – not for the first time, though he guessed he'd always done his damnedest to suppress it – that the fact was black men made *him* hornier than white men or women, which amused him because of how appalled Jewel would be if she knew, but which also made him simmer with a weird kind of deep-down rage.

'How about bicycles?' he asked, seeing Daisy up ahead, right where he'd left her, chained to a black lamppost outside an upscale fashion store.

Tabby laughed. 'Last time I rode a bike, I was ten.'

'It'll come right back,' Cal said, unlocking the padlock. 'And I'll do most of the pedalling.'

'In those?' The other man looked at his platform boots.

'Easy.' Cal patted the front saddle, remembered the guy who'd sold it to him third-hand back in Wilmington talking about it. 'Spring gel,' he said. 'Very comfy.' His new friend swung one leg over the crossbar. 'All aboard then,' he said.

Which was when Cal saw her.

The old bag lady – his stinky old bird – *again*. Stepping along Washington Avenue like she had a right to be there same as anyone else, as if she had a real *life* and a home to go to now, instead of just some lousy bench.

Cal didn't like coincidences.

And what if she was *not* the old derelict she seemed – what if she was an undercover pig?

Except he'd seen her out there a few times now, had *smelled* her, and if she wasn't the real thing, then he was a fucking nun.

'What's up?' Tabby asked, all poised and ready on the back saddle.

Cal stepped closer, took the brown-skinned hand and laid it over his dick.

'Only me,' he said, putting the old woman out of his mind.

'Not only,' the other man said.

His eyes were deep and dark as night, Cal observed close up, and there was something in them that was making him...

Shiver.

44

Mildred, on her way back to her bench, wished she had not seen him again.

Wished, even more, that he had not seen her.

He'd been too far away, on the opposite side of the street, for her to see his eyes, but she had felt them resting on her, no doubt about that, had felt his disrespect, even, she'd fancied, his dislike.

Maybe worse.

All silver again, tonight.

Riding off into the night with that spiffily dressed young black man.

She wondered about that one, about how well he knew her *angel.*

Not well enough, she suspected, and feared for him, though it was hard to say exactly why.

Mildred so hoped to be wrong.

But she did surely wish she had not seen him again.

45

Cal and Tabby were on Alton Road, pedalling smoothly through light traffic.

'How much further?' Tabby asked.

'Just a few blocks,' Cal said over his
shoulder.

'I still don't see why you left this damned
thing so far from the club when it wasn't
even on our way.'

'Her name's Daisy,' Cal said, staying ami-
able. 'I need the exercise.'

'Yeah, yeah,' said Tabby.

'It'll be worth the trip,' Cal said.

'I sure hope so,' the other man said.

He stayed silent for the next five blocks.

Then stayed silent when Cal turned left on
to 16th.

'You OK?' Cal asked.

'Getting bored,' Tabby said.

Two turnings on, and Cal saw the road to
the right where his first *friend* had told him
he lived.

'*We could just as easily go to my place*,' he'd
said.

'*But I have a boat*,' Cal had told him.

'*And I have a comfortable bed*,' the other

man had said, *'just around the corner.'*

'My cruiser is sexier,' Cal had insisted and kept on pedalling.

And the other man had quit arguing and gone with the flow.

Straight on now, past the No Outlet sign.

The sound of the water was tranquil and welcoming.

And of boats, being rocked like babies, their bottoms gently slapped.

Nice and easy tonight.

'Almost there,' Cal said.

46

He had not expected this.

That was a lie. It was *exactly* what he'd anticipated – just not, perhaps, the speed with which it had happened.

He'd thought there would be heat first, like the last time; a little sensuality, some rolling around on the new quilt – which he accepted now that he had bought for fucking, not sleeping.

Not even for fucking, as it turned out.

'Oh,' Tabby had said, when they came down the steps into the tiny, dark, claustrophobic cabin.

Cal, behind him, stooping a little because

169

of his height, had turned on the light and glanced at the small blacked out portholes.

'It's not much, I know,' he'd said modestly.

'That's true enough,' the other man had said.

Which, after all the griping on the way, had made Cal really mad.

The cord had been there, on the bench seat, ready and waiting, looking as harmless as a fat comatose towelling worm.

Cal wasn't sure just how deliberately he'd prepared that earlier, when he'd come for his clothes and face paint, and he didn't suppose it mattered much now.

What mattered was that it had been there.

So that when the anger had risen in him, hot and fast as a rocket, the other man still standing just ahead of him, Cal hadn't had to stop to consider, had just gone for it.

Picked up the cord.

Now.

Smooth and seamless, the motion almost graceful, like a cowboy lassoing a stallion, the white cord looping over the dark head, around the sinewy neck, yanking hard, pulling the man off balance – and that had been so *easy*, because the guy was relaxed, believing Cal wanted him.

Easy.

Just like the last time.

Harder to describe the rest of it, the *killing*, and Cal thought that he might want, in time, to chronicle it in the Epistle, but it wouldn't be easy to put on paper.

A roaring going through him, a power surge, consuming him completely, and he might almost have been some wild, ravening beast or a Harley or maybe even a god-damned combat jet...

Not just a man anymore, in other words. A killer.

Only now, afterwards, he had this *dead* guy at his feet, didn't he, lying sprawled face down on Cal's nice new quilt, which was really messed up because sudden death was like that, all kinds of fluids spilling out, and that made him mad all over again.

You disgust me.

That was what Jewel had said the first time she'd seen him speaking to a black person in the street.

'You *disgust* me,' Cal said now to the dead man.

You know what I have to do now, she'd said to him later, when they were alone.

'You know what I have to do now,' Cal told Tabby.

Who said nothing, did nothing, just lay there in a heap.

What Jewel had done that time was whip him first.

But Cal didn't have a whip.

And after she'd whipped him, she'd kissed and then cleaned the fresh weals on his back and chest and stomach and limbs with chlorine bleach, which had burned him and stabbed at his eyes and nasal passages and choked his throat. And from then on, if he came home with so much as a little dirt on him, she'd order him into the bathtub – and sometimes just the sound of Jewel's voice *ordering* him that way would make him shiver with excitement – but then she'd scrub him until his skin was raw, and sometimes, because she hated body hair as much as stubble, she'd want to shave him, and if he fought her off, he'd always end up getting cut, and then those wounds would have to be disinfected with more bleach. And he knew he should have, could have stopped her, but Jewel was always telling him that if he hurt her, she'd see to it that he'd be locked away in one of those places where *they* lived, and he knew what would become of him then.

So take it like a man, she'd told him.

'So take it like a man,' Cal told Tabby now.

He put on his new gloves and looped one of the masks over his ears, and undressed Tabby, unbuttoned the brown silky shirt and tugged off his D&G loafers, unbuckled the gorgeous belt and unzipped the pants and pulled them off, and he was perspiring as he dragged off the dead man's wine-coloured underpants, but then he remembered – because even then that part of his mind was still working – that his own clothes needed protection, too, didn't they, needed folding away in the boat's dry box. And he was moving real fast, getting it all done, sweat pouring now because it was goddamned hot down here, it was stifling, but he was almost ready for what came next, and he reached for the big plastic two-gallon container and unscrewed the big cap...

The smell made him retch, the way it always did, but the need was filling him, pumping through him, there was no fighting it, and so he picked up the already-human-coated scrubbing brush and knelt down beside the naked man-that-was.

One stroke.

Just *starting* made the fire inside him burn hotter.

Made him unstoppable.

He had to go on, had to, *had* to.

Oh, Jesus, yes.

47

Back home on her bench, Mildred felt cold.

Which was absurd, since she didn't believe she was running a fever, and it was particularly warm tonight and very humid.

She never got sick, could not remember

173

the last time she'd had so much as a sniffle. But tonight, sitting here where she had come to belong, in this tolerant, kindly spot where she often imagined that night itself was wrapping snugly around her, enfolding her, keeping her safe...

Sitting here tonight, she felt sick at heart, and too lonely even to talk to Donny.

Lonely as death.

And so cold.

48

Cal had done.

His worst.

He had stopped a while ago, limp and quivering with exhaustion, and then he'd seen what he had done and gotten sick to his stomach, and when that was finished, too, he'd taken the brush – coated with a thousand, give or take, shreds of the man who had called himself Tabby, coated with his skin, his flesh and his blood – and had begun to punish himself with it.

Diagonal strokes across his chest, from his left shoulder – bypassing his heart because of his tattoo – down to his upper abdomen.

Raking himself.

Too weak to do the job properly, the way

Jewel would have.

And then he stopped doing it at all, be-coming *aware* again.

Of time passing.

Of the dead man on the quilt at his feet.

'One hundred and one things to do with a dead Tabby,' he said out loud, para-phrasing the title of some old bestseller, he thought.

And felt suddenly appalled by his own flip-pancy.

More appalled by that, it seemed to him, than by his deed.

Though maybe that was the only way he could deal with what still needed to be done.

Best not to think too much, he decided, about any of this. Neither about the killing nor the stealing of the hundred and eighty bucks in Tabby-the-cheapskate's Gucci wal-let (he'd considered briefly helping himself to the man's Okamato condoms, but then, for some reason, that idea had repelled him, besides which Cal was an 'America's Most Trusted' Trojan guy himself).

Best not to think about that either.

Most of all, not about the premeditation of it all.

Not just the cord left ready, nor the rest of his paraphernalia, but also the fact that he had already thought through what to do next.

Better prepared than last time, but still an

imperfect plan.

He could be caught out, found out, at any point.

Dangerous stuff.

Fool's luck the last time.

He took a long slug from a bottle of Bombay Sapphire that he'd been keeping since Wilmington for a special occasion, and then he rolled the body in the quilt, took two lengths of nylon dock line from the dry box to secure the bundle and felt immense relief as the dead man's head disappeared from view – his feet and ankles less weird, less *disturbing* to look at, somehow, almost laughable and certainly pathetic, poor bastard.

His anger at Tabby was almost all gone now.

The last time, he'd taken *Baby* out afterwards, and that had been some kind of a miracle of amateur's luck, because so far as he knew no one had taken a scrap of notice when he'd started the engine in the middle of the night, and also because it was tough navigating safely in darkness, staying within the channels dredged and marked by the Coast Guard to keep boats from running aground in the shallow waters and constantly shifting seabed all around Miami. Cal had given thanks that night for many things: mostly, though, for the few hours of tuition he'd bought along with the cruiser, and also for the fact that his brain was a whole lot sharper than he'd ever realized – certainly than Jewel had ever given him credit for.

You had to do a lot more than learn how your boat worked; you had to remember that the rules of the oceans and of Biscayne Bay and the Intracoastal Waterway and the Port of Miami were made to keep you and other ocean-goers in one piece. You had to watch out for the weather, and for great ships and multimillion-dollar yachts and sailboats, and swimmers and dolphins and goddamned protected manatees – most all, you had to watch out for the Coast Guard and other marine patrols.

For the *law*.

Especially when you were carrying a freshly murdered body on board.

It seemed to Cal, thinking back, that when he'd started out on that earlier journey, he'd been planning on heading right out to sea and dumping the body into the depths. And he'd certainly started out that way, moving through the waters without a hitch, right under the noses of all the Star Island billionaires and even slipping all calm and nice as pie through Government Cut – his face and hair still all silver, *and* with a dead man aboard, if you please...

And then he'd seen the rowboat, lit up for just a moment or two by a scrap of moonlight, tied up to a sailboat anchored out in the middle of nowhere, and no one seeming to keep watch except maybe God, and Cal guessed He must have been looking the other way as he'd dropped his fluke anchor ('lower the damn thing,' his teacher had cautioned him, 'don't ever throw it') and had swum across to the rowboat and cut it loose with his Leatherman knife.

Making the small pink-painted boat all his own.

It had felt like a brainwave at the time, he remembered that now, though the *doing* of it all had almost killed him; the tension of it all, and the sheer strength it had taken to secure the little boat to *Baby* so he could weigh anchor again and move farther out to sea and go about the real business of washing down the body and then heaving its dead weight up and over the side of the cruiser. And the physical strain had made him vomit, had made his heart pound so hard he'd believed he might die, but he'd survived.

Not just smarter then, tougher too.

He almost wished he could tell Jewel about it.

Almost.

It mightn't have worked out the way it had. The guy might have missed the rowboat altogether, or he might have capsized it or even smashed it, but then he'd have sunk to the bottom anyway, Cal figured, so it was a kind of win-win situation.

Kind of.

And it had worked out.

This time, he was playing it safer. He had a change of clothes – black T-shirt and grey shorts and sneakers – eye make-up remover for his silver mascara, soap and moisturizer for his face and the rest. He had latched and fastened the door at the top of the steps – not that a padlock would have kept out the cops if someone had called them, but Cal was an optimistic kind of guy a lot of the time.

Maybe a bit of a gambler too.

Right now, for instance, he was gambling on his dead Tabby staying safely out of trouble on *Baby* while he went, by foot, to find himself another little-bitty boat, and he knew he'd seen a couple of dinghies tied up to bigger boats at the back of some apartment buildings just a few blocks south.

Bingo.

Not one, but two candidates for his purposes. One more expensive looking than the other, so more likely to be alarm-protected. The second a whole lot less special, with a pair of oars on show as well as its outboard motor – and not even tied up to another boat, just tethered to the mooring.

A breeze.

He waited a little while, watching and

listening for trouble.

All quiet.

Decision made, he crouched to untie the line, and suddenly it occurred to him that maybe he could keep this boat, maybe toss Tabby overboard into the deep after all and sail *Baby* away with this neat little dink for extra insurance.

But a plan was a plan. And if it all worked out same as last time, Cal found that he was itching to see what went down when this one was found.

If he was found. He might not be, the dinghy might be hit by a big wave and Tabby might sink without trace, which would be OK, too, in its way. Safer, without question, for Cal.

But not as interesting.

The high kept on boosting him all the way to the finish, a constantly growing sense of achievement like nothing else before, better even than the last time because the tension and that touch of beginner's luck had taken the edge off that accomplishment –but this time he *knew* what he was doing.

Paddling the dinghy through the dark water back to Flamingo Marina and *Baby*, then hitching the line to a cleat.

'Cleat,' he said out loud. 'Cleat-clit.' Thinking about turning the words into a tap-dance kind of tune, the way he had with the

'Epistle of the Apostles' – 'cleat-clit, clit-cleat' – but this was no time for singing or dancing, this was a time for silent concentration as he got back on board the cruiser, and oh, man, he was turning into such a *sailor*, and maybe he could consider renting himself out as a deckhand.

Deck-sex-hand.

Except time was passing, night wouldn't last forever, and day started early in marinas, and Tabby had to be off *Baby* and floating away before dawn, so Cal gathered up his new brilliant discipline, cast off from the dock, started the cruiser's engine and reversed carefully out, and if he so much as brushed another boat's fender right now, he might be in a fucking holding cell by breakfast-time...

But he did not. And after that, navigating his way through the markers in the bay, passing under the East Bridge of Julia Tuttle Causeway, staying slow and steady, controlling the impulse for speed, taking *Baby* around La Gorce Island and under the 79th Street Causeway, heading for Baker's Haulover Inlet this time, because getting through Government Cut unimpeded really *had* been more than a little fluky, and Haulover Cut was choppier, but otherwise safer, at least for him; and after all that, after dropping anchor out in the Atlantic, the greatest dangers of all were to his back and arms –

and to his mind, perhaps, most of all – when he had to drag another dead weight up the friggin steps and unroll the quilt, exposing that naked, wounded *deadness*, and then hose him down on deck before heaving him over the side into the dinghy, but he got the job done, he really got it *done*.

'Who's a dumb-ass now, Jewel?' Cal yelled into the remains of the night.

No one except the birds and fish to hear him.

And maybe God.

49

Grace came downstairs with Joshua a few minutes after seven to find Claudia's note propped against a marmalade jar on the kitchen table.

Dearest Grace,

I reached my decision to go back in the middle of the night, and knew that if I waited to talk it over with you, I might change my mind, and then I might never get up the nerve to do the right thing. I love you all, and thank you from the bottom of my heart.

Your Claudia.

Grace burst into tears, which started Joshua off, too.

'Oh, I'm sorry, sweetheart,' she told him, and stopped her own weeping to comfort him. 'It's OK, baby, Mommy's fine.' She wiped her eyes with the back of one hand, then kissed the tip of his nose, which often made him laugh.

No laughter now, neither in her son nor herself.

She waited until he was soothed, then put him in his highchair, picked up the phone and pressed the speed dial key for her sister's cell phone.

Switched off.

50

Cal didn't like the way he was feeling now.

Real shaken up. Nowhere near as good about himself as the last time.

No singing in the blood.

This was different. Premeditated and, perhaps partly because of that, starting to feel more than a little scary.

Wicked.

He had cleaned and cleaned *Baby* while they were still at sea, and except for the scrubbing brush, all the evidence was gone, sunk deep in the ocean same as the first time, and after he'd finished that hard labour, he'd considered that maybe this was the moment to take the cruiser someplace new. But in the end he'd brought her back through Haulover to Flamingo because it was, after all, paid for. And because even if he'd aimed at some really distant destination, he'd have had to stop for fuel in a bunch of places, and each time he'd be risking attracting attention to himself, and so far as he'd been aware there had been no one around last night when he'd cycled in with Tabby, so it made no sense...

Not that anything much *did* make sense anymore.

He couldn't really remember now if it ever had, and most of his coherent thinking had been done out there on the water, all of it gone now, intelligence being squeezed out by pain.

Not really the physical kind, that wasn't what was getting to him. The stabbing in his neck and shoulders and spine was no more than he deserved, though the pain had been bad enough to stop him from getting off *Baby* yet again and going back to his hideaway.

The stink of the bleach down below in the small cabin was worse than the pain, he thought, because it brought it all back. The memory of what he'd done, and what had been done to him. It all seemed one now, one overwhelming agony cut too deep in his mind for him to reach and eradicate it.

Only one way he knew of – short of killing himself, and Cal didn't want to do that, not yet at least – only one thing that would blot out those memories, those feelings, for a time.

So Cal picked up the big brush that was intended for scrubbing decks, its hard bristles layered now with the shreds of three humans, and he pulled off the clothes he'd changed into earlier, after he'd finished...

Don't think, he told himself.

All the images were still there, scalding his mind.

'Please,' he said, beginning to weep. 'I don't want to.'

You have to, Jewel said, inside his head.

So Cal picked up the brush and did it again, opened up his own still-fresh wounds, and then he took his T-shirt and stuffed it in his mouth to muffle the screams that would come.

When he picked up the container of bleach and poured every drop that was left over himself.

51

Sam was in the office at eight fifteen when his phone vibrated with a new text.

From Mildred, telling him that she'd seen the silver angel again.

IN FACT, I'VE SEEN HIM TWICE –
THOUGH EARLY MONDAY MORNING HE
WAS NOT SILVER AT ALL.

'Think I'll grab ten minutes later on,' Sam told Martinez. 'Check this out.'

'She's an old lady,' Martinez said. 'Might be seeing stuff.'

'More down-to-earth than a lot of us,' Sam said.

With Claudia's phone still switched off, Grace didn't know what to do for the best.

She felt so badly for her sister, heading back to what would inevitably be a traumatic confrontation, travelling alone and surely filled with all kinds of trepidation and fears. Yet Grace felt proud of her, too, for reaching that decision and acting on it right away; she accepted that speed and the rejection of more procrastination must have seemed the only way for Claudia.

Proud, and afraid for her, too.

What Grace wanted was to be able to tell Claudia that she was proud of her courage, because she knew her sister well enough to realize that a little approval right now might help her just a little, but for now Grace could not even do that much for her, could only wait.

The house felt strangely empty with her gone. Which was, she decided abruptly, a good reason for her to get right back to the process of returning to work; anything to take her mind off Claudia for a while – and there were still a few more hurdles to jump before she could actually hang up her shingle again, get back to doing what she loved, what she was good at.

The phone rang and she picked it up quickly.

'Grace, it's Magda.'

'Magda, you're psychic,' Grace said. 'I've just been sitting here wondering if I ought to have a couple of sessions with you before I start seeing patients again.'

'Would you like to arrange that now?' asked Magda, getting straight down to business, which was one of the many things Grace admired about her psychologist friend.

'Sounds good to me,' Grace said.

Her sister was in pain, yet she was about to take a major step forward.

Silver linings, she guessed.

52

'Sam, did you guys hear it all the way down there?'

Saul's call at nine fifteen to Sam's cell phone came less than ten minutes after the police department's phones had all started ringing off the hook.

There had been a third explosion. In broad daylight this time, but at sea again, somewhere further north.

'We didn't hear a thing,' Sam told his brother, 'but we're starting to hear all about it now.'

'It was pretty loud up here,' Saul said.

'You and Dad OK?' Sam checked.

'Sure,' Saul said. 'Want me to call Grace?'

'I just spoke to her,' Sam told him. 'But I'm sure she'd be happy to hear your voice anyway. Claudia left in the early hours.'

'So soon?' Saul was surprised.

'Homesick, I guess,' Sam said. 'Listen, bro, I gotta deal with stuff here.'

'Be safe,' Saul said.

'Love you,' said Sam.

Confirmation came in ten minutes later that the new explosion had happened on another boat – out of Miami Beach jurisdiction again – somewhere off Dania Beach.

There was more solid news, too, on the subject of the Leehy yacht.

'Turns out it was stolen by the maid's ex-boyfriend–' Martinez had it hot off the grapevine – 'with some nutso idea of torching it – who the fuck knows why – and the guy ended up frying himself along with it.'

'So no connection with Dania or Lauderdale,' said Sam. 'Unless it sparked off the kids again.'

'Not a yacht this time either,' Beth Riley reported. 'Some kind of speedboat.'

Sam checked his watch and stood up. 'I'm going to grab a word with Mildred.'

'I'm backed up here,' Martinez said, shuffling papers.

'Back in fifteen to twenty,' Sam said.

'I don't know why I should feel so relieved to see you,' Mildred told Sam, 'and to get this off my chest.' She shook her head. 'I still don't even know why I feel he's so important. I probably shouldn't be giving him another thought.'

'But you are,' Sam said. 'Which means something in my book.'

She'd invited him to sit, most of the pedes-

189

trian traffic flowing past the bench heading for the beach. She looked tired, her blue eyes less sharp than usual and wreathed in puckers of weariness.

'I saw him early this morning on the corner of Washington and 9th, just after one thirty.' Mildred raised both wrists, showing her two watches. 'No problem being sure of the time.'

She told him about the man's sharply dressed companion, and about her instinctive concerns – which she hoped had been irrational – for the second stranger.

'They looked to me as if they'd been to a party, or maybe to one of those nightclubs, as if maybe they'd been dancing.'

'But you didn't feel that they were a couple,' Sam said.

'A real couple?' Mildred shook her head. 'They looked brand new to me.' She thought some more about it. 'They were walking south along Washington when our silver friend stopped to pick up this tandem – one of those nice old bicycles for two, you know? It was definitely his, not the other way around, because he had it chained to a lamppost, and he was the one who unlocked it – and I can't be sure, but I don't think his friend had ever seen it before. And then off they went together.' She paused again. 'I'd probably have thought it quaint if he didn't chill me so.'

'Which way did they go, did you notice?' Sam asked.

'They rode north,' she said.

'Do you think he saw you?'

'Again, I can't be sure,' Mildred said, 'but yes, I'd say so.'

Sam looked around. It was overcast again, humidity high, rain forecast to blow in later, but there were plenty of people on the beach and promenade and behind them back on Ocean Drive.

'I hope you're not worrying about me, Samuel,' Mildred said.

'I don't suppose,' Sam said, 'you'd consider spending a few nights inside?'

'I don't do shelters,' Mildred said, 'unless there's a big hurricane blowing.'

Sam pondered. With no evidence that this guy was guilty of anything more sinful than being another SoBe character, it was hard to know what to do for the best.

'I know a place – not a shelter – where they owe me a favour or two.'

'What kind of a place?' Mildred was suspicious.

'A bed and breakfast.' He was making this up as he went along, hoping he was good enough to fool her, but not one bit sure of that.

'And where is this place?'

He had to make it right if Proud Mildred was to agree.

'Over on Alton,' he said. 'It's called Freddie's.'

Mildred's face creased into a friendly scowl. 'You took a little too long, Detective. They don't owe you a dime at that place. You're thinking of paying for my room, and don't you lie to me, Samuel Becket.'

'I just want you someplace safe,' Sam said, 'till we can talk to this silver dude.' Her text came back to him. 'You said he wasn't silver when you saw him early Monday.'

'That's right,' Mildred said, 'but I still can't tell you any more about him. It was dark. He walked past my bench, and I knew it was the same man, and he made my skin crawl, but he looked like a million other young men in the night.'

'Still skinny?'

'Definitely that. Not so tall, though, without those foolish things on his feet.'

'Anything else?'

'He wore a baseball cap,' Mildred said, 'but I can't even tell you the colour, except that was dark too. I was trying not to let him see I'd even noticed him. I felt safer having him think I was sleeping.' She paused. 'You think he might have killed the man in the boat?'

'I don't know. Probably not.' Sam looked back at her. 'Do you?'

She shrugged. 'How would I know? I'm just an old bag lady.'

'You got the lady part right.' Sam took her

hand and kissed it, saw her weathered cheeks grow warm. 'Will you do me a favour and go to Freddie's?'

'No, Samuel, I will not,' she said. 'But I thank you for your kindness.'

He sighed. 'If you change your mind—'

'Then you'll hear from me.'

Sam's cell phone rang and he answered, listened briefly to Elliot Sanders, off-duty but with news he felt Sam and Martinez needed to hear. 'Thank you,' he said. 'We'll be there.'

Mildred was watching him intently. 'What is it, Samuel?'

'I have to go,' he said.

'Something bad?' She saw his grimness. 'Is it another death?'

Sam was up on his feet. 'Do you have any plans, Mildred?'

'No, sir,' she said. 'If you want me, I'll be around.'

On impulse, he stooped, kissed her cheek.

'Stay safe,' he said.

53

That made Cal burn.

The kiss.

That stinky old bird.

He'd had a bad feeling about her last night. The way she'd looked at him when he and Tabby had gotten on board Daisy.

The way she was *there*.

He was only here now because he'd been on his way back to the fleapit and figured he ought to pick up a fresh pint of milk and something for his pain – and it had been as much as he could manage to get himself off *Baby* and out of the marina without crying out and having people staring at him. And right after he'd bought the milk and extra strength Excedrin, and a white loaf and a jar of Skippy creamy peanut butter for consolation, some kind of weird fascination had taken him close enough to the cop shop to smell the jokers coming in and out of the big white building, detectives and uniforms and witnesses and lawyers and criminals and more cops.

He'd seen one of them, in plain clothes, stride out, tall and purposeful, and head over the street and on down 11th, crossing over, and for all Cal knew he might have been going right to his very own alleyway and the pisshole, so he'd waited a few moments, for safety's sake, then followed.

The other man had passed the alley without so much as a sideways glance.

Kept right on going.

Heading towards Lummus Park.

Where *she* lived.

Which had made Cal want to go on following, because he had a *feeling*, and he'd known he should have gone back to the dump instead, but he'd felt like the other guy and the tramp were some kind of magnet, sucking him towards them...

And then there they were, like bosom buddies or even mom and son.

Which had made him want to puke.

And then he had *kissed* her.

54

Miami-Dade had been on the scene for quite a while – the techs moving briskly about their business because the skies were threatening rain and, therefore, the crime scene – when Sam and Martinez arrived just after ten forty.

Sanders was already there, after the courtesy heads-up he'd received from Dr Mike Dietrich, a poker buddy and the on-call ME.

'Dietrich was right.' Sanders, a family man who lived about a mile north on Collins, looked incongruous in a Hawaiian-style shirt that billowed in the breeze over a pair of XXL black shorts. 'Looks a whole lot like our 10th Street guy.'

They were on the beach in Surfside, just a handful of blocks from the Adani home. Which might be meaningful but was, considering the vagaries of the ocean, probably pure coincidence, Sam and Martinez had already agreed, since the pair of guys who'd found the dinghy and its gruesome cargo had happened upon it while they'd been messing about on their own Sunfish a little way out from the beach.

Having seen what lay inside, they'd freaked first, then toughed it out for the same reasons that had made Joe Myerson pull in the rowboat bearing Sanjiv Adani's body, had tied it up to their boat and towed it to shore.

Two young men, named Carson and Kahn, neither of whom would ever completely expunge from their memories what they'd seen this day.

'African-American, probably late twenties, naked, strangled with a ligature and taken from behind. Nothing to help ID him, and no wedding band mark' – Sanders pulled a

pack of Marlboro from his breast pocket –
'but it's the injuries on the body that are just
too damned similar to ignore.'

Sam looked towards the Miami-Dade investigators and their team. 'We OK to take a
look?'

'Help yourselves.' Sanders put the pack
back in his pocket with a sigh, and walked
with them.

Another beach, another victim, another set
of detectives and crime scene technicians,
but the whole scene was horrifically and
depressingly *déjà vu*.

'Nice,' Martinez said. 'Someone's done
this twice now.'

'At least,' Sam said grimly.

The possibilities of a copycat seeming unlikely, with details of Adani's wounds as yet
unreleased to the media.

'Getting a taste for it,' Sanders said.

The thought made Sam feel mad as well as
queasy.

And more than a little afraid.

David had once told him that any man
who could see stuff as bad as this would be a
damned fool if it did not make him afraid.

'Afraid for humanity,' he'd said.

Looking down into the dinghy now, Sam
knew what his father had meant.

And knew, too, that there was one really
ugly thing that he needed to take care of just
as soon as it could be arranged, something

he'd much sooner have avoided.

'We need to have Mildred take a look.' He'd already brought Martinez up to speed with Mildred's sighting of her silver 'angel' and his new pal. 'Lord knows she's jumpy enough about him already.'

'Old lady like that,' Martinez agreed, 'shouldn't have to see this.'

Sam stooped again for another close look, noted that there were, thankfully, fewer bloody striations on this victim's face than on his torso. 'Let's ask the team for some head shots and see if they put him in the ball park for her.'

'If this is the guy,' Martinez said, 'I think Mildred should come off the streets until we have the bastard.'

'Stubborn lady,' Sam said. 'Easier said.'

55

Grace, who seldom took Joshua out for walks in his stroller when the South Florida summer sun was blazing down, was standing in the front doorway wondering if the rain was going to hold off long enough for them to cross Kane Concourse, get to the French bakery and dry cleaners on the East Island and home again, when the phone rang.

She hesitated, listened to the machine picking up.

'Grace, it's me.'

The voice was a whisper, but it sounded like Claudia, which couldn't be right, since she was still en route to Seattle, but if her plane had seatback phones...

Grace shut the front door, abandoned the baby and ran for the phone.

'Grace, it's Claudia, please pick—'

She snatched it up. 'Sis, I'm here. Are you all right?'

'Not all right.' Claudia was barely audible. 'Grace, I'm at Papa's.'

'Why?' Confusion and the beginnings of anger sent Grace's voice higher. 'What the hell happened?'

'Just *listen*, for God's sake.' Still that inaudible, almost muffled voice. 'I think something bad's going on here.'

'What kind of stuff?' Realization hit Grace. 'Is it Jerome?'

'Grace, you need to—'

The line clicked and died.

'I'm on my way,' Sam told her from the Saab. 'I'll be home in ten.'

Alvarez had told him to take the day, temporarily turning the Adani lead over to Martinez and assigning Beth Riley to the case till Sam's return, their first task as temporary partners to check which nightclubs had been open last night near to where Mildred had seen the two men climbing aboard the tandem.

'I keep trying to get back to her,' Grace said, 'but her phone's switched off.'

'And you've tried your father's number again?'

'Still no answer.' Grace felt sick with fear. 'Sam, I have such a bad feeling about this.'

Sam trusted his wife's 'bad' feelings. 'I'm going to make a call to the Cook County Sheriff's Office,' he said. 'Ask them to check it out.'

'I have to get out to the airport,' Grace said. 'I have to get to Chicago, find out what's going on.'

'If anyone's going to Chicago,' Sam said, 'it'll be me.'

'She's my—'

'No argument,' Sam said.

56

Claudia had known as soon as the other woman had opened the front door.

This visit was a bad idea.

Jerome's mother was dishevelled, clad in an ugly velour dressing gown with a zipper pulled all the way to the neck, her feet encased in what looked like bed socks. No obvious physical resemblance to her son that Claudia could see.

They had never met, but the older woman had seemed to know her immediately.

And her eyes had filled with dislike.

Jerome's mother for sure.

'I'm Claudia.' She'd steeled herself, suppressed her impulse to turn tail, had put out her hand instead.

'Yes,' Roxanne Lucca had said.

She had declined the handshake, but taken a step back into her house.

'You better come in.'

Last chance to run.

But Claudia was done with cowardice.

So she had stepped inside the house.

57

There had been no answer, Sam told Grace, when the Cook County patrol cops had called at the Lucca house in Melrose Park.

'No 911 call, and no external signs of trouble,' he said.

Nowhere near enough to go on, in other words, for them to break in.

'The next flight out of MIA's at one thirty,' Grace told Sam. 'We can be in Chicago by four, local time.'

'Not "we".' Sam was still adamant. 'Like I told you.'

'We could drop Joshua at your dad's.'

'We could, but we won't.' Sam was halfway up the staircase, unfastening his holster as he went, since much as he might have liked to be armed, there was no way he was going to play those kinds of games at MIA or any-place out of jurisdiction and end up in a world of new trouble.

'That makes no sense.' Grace followed him into the bedroom, agitatedly watched him lock away the Glock. 'Claudia's depending on me.'

'She's depending on *us*,' Sam reminded her. 'So you can get this straight, Gracie. Whatever's happening inside your father's house, whether it's Frank or his wife or Cooper behind it' – he checked his wallet, credit cards, ID – 'there's no way on this earth you're going in there.'

'Then let me at least be there. I can wait outside.'

'And what if Claudia calls back and there's no one here?' He paused on his way back to the door, took her face in both his hands and kissed her mouth. 'I know it's hard as hell to be the one doing the waiting, sweetheart, but I'm going to be on that flight alone.'

Not many nightclubs did open off-season in

South Beach on Tuesday nights, so it hadn't taken Martinez and Riley long to pinpoint just two in the immediate area, Hot-Hot-Hot and Menagerie, their plan to take the cropped head shots of the new victim to both places later.

After they'd shown them to Mildred.

The photographs were still pretty grisly for all Miami-Dade's efforts, but the best they could manage.

Except that there was no sign of Mildred in Lummus Park or on the beach, neither near her bench nor anyplace around.

'Maybe she's lying low because she's scared,' Riley said.

'More likely because we're not Sam,' Martinez said.

They hung around Ocean Drive for a while, and while Riley checked out the near-by restroom, Martinez tried sending her a text, and then they waited another five minutes.

No show.

Sam called Grace just before boarding.

'Any more from Claudia?'

'Not a thing,' Grace told him. 'Her phone's still switched off and no answer at the house.'

'How're you and Joshua holding up?'

'Don't worry about us, we're fine.'

'I've been wondering,' Sam said, 'if you

oughtn't to be telling Daniel.'

'Me too,' Grace said. 'But there's nothing he could do except go crazy.'

'If it were me,' Sam said, 'I'd want to be told.'

'Told what? That Claudia let us think she was going home to him, but went to Chicago instead? How could we do that without raising the other issues?'

'Not our place,' Sam agreed. 'Let's wait.'

'At least till you find out what's going on,' Grace said. 'Or she calls me again.'

Mildred could not easily have explained why she hadn't wanted to speak to those two cops. Neither of them were strangers to her, after all, but then she'd always – even while Donny had still been alive – been picky about who she chose to spend time with.

Time being the only commodity she had to barter these days.

Samuel Becket was different. Before him, there'd been that pleasant young Officer Valdez, and she'd had no objection to passing the time of day with him on occasion, but her relationship with Detective Becket was something else altogether.

'That's it, precisely,' she said to her dead fiancé. 'We do *relate* to each other.'

Not that Detective Martinez had ever disrespected her, or that nice enough red-headed young woman who had been with him this afternoon.

But Samuel Becket had given her a telephone.

Samuel Becket had wanted her to go to a *hotel*, had wanted to pay for that out of his own hard-earned money so that she could be safe. And not just – she was sure about that – because he thought she might be some kind of eye-witness.

No one since Donny had truly given a damn about Mildred Bleeker.

'Not that I've allowed them to,' she told him now. 'To be fair.'

A boy aged about fourteen, in foolish-looking baggy pants and a baseball cap, passed by the trees where she was still hiding in case the detectives came back, saw her talking to herself and rolled his eyes.

'Weirdo,' Mildred heard him say.

And then she realized, suddenly, the real reason behind her reluctance to talk to Becket's colleagues. It was because she was afraid of exactly why Samuel had not been out there, as usual, with his partner.

She was scared that something bad might have happened to him.

'Neurosis,' she told herself, because he might just have influenza, or be working on some other case, or even simply be taking a day off.

But Samuel Becket had asked her, just this morning, if she'd be around later.

And then he had kissed her on the cheek.

So neurotic or not, Mildred was anxious that there might be some bad reason for his not having been here with Detective Martinez this same afternoon.

And the truth was she didn't want to know what that reason might be.

Not until she had to.

58

'I'm at O'Hare,' Sam told Grace at 4.05 p.m., moving fast through the arrivals concourse towards the exit.

'Thank God,' she said. 'No news here.'

'I'm almost at the cab line,' he said. 'Be there soon as.'

'Have you called the Sheriff's office yet?'

'Jury's still out on exactly when I tell them I'm here.'

Outside it was grey and windy, a heck of a lot cooler than Miami, but still pretty humid. The line was shorter than it might have been, and Sam positioned himself behind a group of four businessmen discussing their dinner plans for the evening ahead.

'Are you sure that's such a good idea?' Grace said.

'I'm not forgetting my history,' Sam assured her. 'But if no one opens the door to me at your dad's house, I want the option of finding my own way in. Get in and get Claudia safely out – then call for back-up if necessary.'

'I love you,' Grace said, trusting his instincts and too damned grateful for his motives to risk any argument. 'So much.'

The line was moving swiftly, plenty of cabs flowing in and out, and the talk ahead of Sam was still of slabs of baby-back ribs, though nothing, he knew, was likely to spark any appetite in him until he had good news for his wife.

'You try and stay calm,' he told her. 'Kiss the baby for me.'

'You just stay safe,' she told him back.

South of Franklin Park, a couple of miles from his destination, Sam's cell phone rang, startling him out of the kind of blank zone that the drab semi-suburban cab ride had seemed to damp over his brain.

'Do me a favour, man,' Martinez said. 'No craziness this time, OK?'

'None planned,' Sam told him. 'Any ID from Miami-Dade on the new victim?'

'Nothing yet,' said Martinez. 'And nothing from Mildred yet either. Riley and I went to find her, but if she was around, she wasn't coming out to play.'

The cab pulled up at a red light inter-
section.

'Do me a favour,' Sam said, 'and try again
later.'

'Goes without saying,' Martinez said. 'You
told the Sheriff you're there?'

'Not yet,' Sam said. 'I'm on leave, remember.'

'Yeah,' Martinez said. 'Day off with the
family.'

The lights turned to green, and they were
moving again.

'Do you know,' Sam said, 'that I never even
met my father-in-law before?'

'Sure I know,' Martinez said. 'And from
the sounds of him, you didn't miss much,
though it's always beaten the hell out of me
how a man like that could get himself a
daughter like Grace.'

'Tell me about it,' said Sam.

David and Saul had just arrived at the house
on Bay Harbor Island.

'Sam didn't need to tell you,' Grace said.
'How much do you know?'

'Enough,' David said, 'about your so-called
stepbrother.'

'Still,' Grace said, 'this really wasn't necessary, I'm perfectly fine.'

'You won't be perfectly fine,' David said,
'till you know Claudia's OK.'

'And Sam's home again,' Saul added.

She hugged them one at a time.

'Glad to have you,' she said. 'As always.'

Sam had his cab driver drop him off at the end of the street.

It looked nicer than he'd anticipated – though he'd had no good reason to expect drabness, since the misery of the young life that had coloured Grace's personal descriptions of Melrose Park had happened, for the most part, in another house on another street.

Here, the sidewalks were well-maintained, and the houses too, with cared-for front yards, plentiful trees and flowers.

Sam paid off the driver, pulled out his phone, waited till the car had moved away and then called Grace again.

'Almost there,' he said.

'Your dad and Saul are here. You didn't need to tell them.'

'I didn't want you being alone.' Sam started strolling. 'Don't worry if you don't hear from me for a while.'

'Even a sniff of trouble,' Grace said, 'swear you'll call for help.'

'No heroics, sweetheart, I swear.'

He ended the call, went on up the road.

'How long should we wait, do you think,' Grace asked David, 'before we call the Sheriff's office?'

Saul was on the floor in the den, playing with Joshua.

Plenty of laughter happening.

'He hasn't even gone inside yet,' David said. 'Let's not look for trouble.'

'Jerome Cooper is trouble,' Grace said. 'I was wrong not to let Sam arrest him here.'

'We don't even know if the guy's there,' Saul pointed out. 'He'd have had to have been following Claudia nonstop, which is a stretch, surely?'

'Maybe she knew he'd already gone back,' Grace said. 'Maybe that's why she went there to confront him.' She dropped down on to her knees, and her son gave a throaty chuckle. 'Anyway, our father might have been a bastard, but he's sixty-five years old now, and I can't picture him or his wife as enough of a threat to have had Claudia sounding so scared.'

'Probably this Jerome character then,' David said.

'Who you said is just a creep,' Saul said. 'Which means Sam can probably handle him with one hand tied behind his back.'

'Probably,' Grace said, miserably.

'I say we need to give Sam an hour,' David said.

'I don't think I can possibly wait that long,' Grace said.

'Grab a cuddle with this little guy,' Saul said, and tickled his nephew's belly.

Grace glanced at her father-in-law, noticed for the first time how tired and pale he looked. 'Are you feeling all right?'

'I got a little head cold starting, nothing much.'

'Can I get you something for it?'

'I took already,' David said.

'You should go home,' Grace said. 'Both of you.'

'You should know by now,' David said, 'we're not that easy to get rid of.'

The house was the plainest in the street.

A squat, two-storey structure with a pitched roof, its walls clad in dull brown and grey timber. The kind of house whose frontage resembled a face and abruptly put Sam in mind of the spooky house in the old Amityville Horror movie poster.

He shut the thought right off, threw a glance up at the iron-grey clouds while considering, one more time, the wisdom of calling the cops now, then decided yet again that it would be premature, time-wasting and, more than likely, pointless.

He raised his right hand, rapped twice on the green door.

Got no reply.

He took a few steps back and checked out the path that led around to the rear of the house – saw nothing but a low fence and some shrubs to keep him out – and then he

211

moved back to the door and rapped one more time.

The door opened.

59

Cal was writing in the Epistle.

Cal the Hater. Never more so.

He remembered hoping, when he first bought *Baby*, that his very own boat would sail him into a better future, out of pain and bitterness and hate, of others and of himself.

He'd learned differently.

He was calmer now than he had been earlier, though his back and shoulders and the wounds on his chest still hurt like hell, and he wished he had more gin, but somehow, seeing the cop and the old woman together, the kiss and all, had sent him hurrying back to his dump without even thinking of buying another bottle.

Have I ever written about where I got my liking for gin?

Same place I got my name.

And my Joy-Boy get-up.

From Jewel, of course.

He had time to go on writing a while longer,

because sunset was not until after eight, and he couldn't do what came next till after dark.

No doubting that he was going to have to do it.

Though he wasn't exactly sure yet how.

But it would happen, one way or another. It had to.

60

'Claudia,' Sam said.

She stood just inside the doorway, half of her face obscured by shadow, the visible half tense and pale in the poor light from within.

Sam tried to read the eye he could see, but it was hard to decipher. Except, that was, for the fear.

'Are you all right?' he asked.

She took a breath, then exhaled it in a small sigh.

'Come in,' she said.

'Wouldn't you rather come outside?' Sam asked.

Since that was what he wanted most, and had promised Grace: to get her sister out of this house.

'Please,' Claudia said. 'Come in.'

Nothing so easy then.

'Sure,' Sam said.

He stepped over the threshold into Frank Lucca's home, and the smell hit his nostrils, made him hesitate.

He *almost* saw the figure as the door shut behind him.

Just a fragment of an impression, no more than that, no time for more.

Because the corner of a heavy old gilt lamp struck him, hard, on the right hand side of his head.

And all the lights went out.

61

'I think I should call him,' Grace said.

They'd moved into the kitchen a while back. David and Saul sat at the table, drinking coffee; Joshua sat in his playpen, gazing at Woody, who lay in his bed near the doggy door watching Grace as she paced back and forth over the stone tiles.

'It's been no real time at all,' David said.

'You have to give them a chance to talk,' Saul said.

'First meeting for them, after all,' said David.

'But if they're just talking,' Grace said, 'and Claudia's fine, then why hasn't Sam called me by now to let me know?'

Father and son looked at each other.

'Maybe no one's home,' Saul said.

'No one answered when the police called,' David said.

'So Sam's probably not even made it inside yet,' Saul said.

'Would you both stop,' said Grace. 'We all know something's wrong.'

'Nothing Sam can't cope with, I'll bet,' Saul said.

'I'm going to call,' Grace said, and picked up the phone from the table.

'You might interrupt a delicate moment,' David said. 'Who knows?'

'Dad's right,' Saul said.

'I know it's hard,' David said.

About to snap at them, Grace stopped herself, knowing that they were very probably right. Because whatever Sam might have walked into, he was, after all, an experienced homicide detective, and the last thing he needed in the middle of *something* was his damned fool wife calling to check on him.

'I just wish he'd call,' she said lamely.

'You're not alone there,' David said.

62

'Sam.'

The voice sounded as if it was coming at him through fog.

'Sam!'

He told himself to open his eyes, found that he was lying on his back on a linoleum floor in a narrow hallway, and even in the dim lighting, he could see that the ceiling overhead was stained, perhaps by nicotine; though the stench in his nostrils was not cigarette smoke, neither fresh nor stale.

His hands were tied behind his back, and his eyes were stinging, and he badly needed to cough, to rid himself of the stink that was in his throat too.

Pain when he coughed, in his head and right across his chest.

'Shit,' he said in protest, then coughed again. 'God *damn*.'

'Sam, are you OK?'

Same voice. Female. He turned his head, peered through the semi-darkness and saw his sister-in-law on the floor about a dozen feet away, trussed up to a radiator.

'Thank Christ,' Claudia said. 'I thought

she'd killed you.'

'She?' Sam struggled for a moment, trying to gather his scrambled thoughts, then remembered, abruptly, exactly where he was and remembered the figure, too, just before the pain.

'Roxanne,' Claudia said. 'She's gone. A while ago.'

Sam's mind sharpened up a little. 'What about Jerome? And your dad?'

'I never got to see either of them.' Claudia's eyes grew fearful. 'I don't even know if they're here. I only saw her.'

'Nice woman.' Sam listened for a moment, heard nothing, hoped that meant the house was empty, then tried sitting up and groaned with the pain. 'Not big on welcomes, is she?'

Claudia began to cry. 'I'm so sorry, Sam. When she let me in, she seemed a little hostile, but she was wearing this old robe, and she just didn't look *dangerous*. I never dreamed...'

'It's OK.' Sam tried sitting up again, made it this time.

'She took me into that room' – Claudia nodded towards a closed door to Sam's right – 'and I told her about Jerome, and she told me to wait while she got my father.' Her tears were still flowing. 'And I had a feeling something wasn't right, so I phoned Grace, but then she came back and she was dressed, and she had a big *knife*, and she dragged me out here and tied me up.' She spoke rapidly, afraid of someone coming. 'But then when you got here, she untied me and said that if I didn't get you to come inside, she'd kill me and then go after Grace and that she wouldn't stop there.'

Sam tucked down his chin, needing to check himself out, saw that his shirt had been ripped open and that there was blood all over his chest, told himself quickly that however much it hurt, the damage couldn't be too bad because the bleeding was just oozing, not pumping.

Yet that was where the acrid stench was coming from, from his goddamned *chest*. 'What the hell did she do to me?'

'Sam, I'm so sorry,' Claudia said again.

He fought to make sense of what was going on, to take some kind of control of the situation. 'Are you all right?' He screwed up his eyes to get a better look at her, saw that despite her pallor and fear she appeared uninjured. 'Did she hurt you?'

'No,' she said. 'I'm OK.'

'Good,' Sam said.

First things first.

He listened for another moment – still nothing – then shuffled across the linoleum until he was as close as he could get to Claudia, and saw that she'd been bound with some kind of twine, probably the same stuff that was tied round his own wrists. 'Can you turn a little, so I can try to get you free?'

Claudia tried, but found she'd been tied up too tightly to move. 'If you get your hands up a little way,' she suggested, 'maybe I could try untying the knots with my teeth.'

'I don't know if—'

'Grace and I both have strong teeth,' Claudia said. 'Our mom did, too.'

Sam couldn't recall Grace ever having so much as a filling. 'Go for it.'

It took some time, cost her some pain and a few more tears of frustration before the twine was loose enough for Sam to extricate his hands.

'Good job,' he said, rubbed them swiftly, then set about freeing her from the radiator pipe.

'Can we get out of here?' Claudia said. 'Please.'

Sam glanced back down at the mess on his chest, tentatively touched one of the bloody wounds – and knew, suddenly, exactly what the stench was.

'Jesus,' he said, totally thrown.

Which was when they both heard the sound.

Moaning.

63

'That's it,' Grace said. 'Not a minute longer.'

No one was arguing.

She picked up the phone. 'If Sam doesn't answer, I'm calling the Sheriff's office.'

'Go on,' David said, rubbing his right temple, willing away his headache.

Grace hit the speed dial number.

Sam heard his cell phone ringing.

Not out here in the hallway.

He turned, realized it was coming from behind him, from a room at the back of the house. 'You stay here,' he told Claudia softly.

'Be careful,' she whispered.

He opened the door cautiously, saw a kitchen, lighter than the hallway but still drab with sludge green linoleum on the floor, formica and plastic all over.

The ringing was coming from the waste bin.

Sam opened the lid, plunged his hand through coffee grounds, damp paper and unwashed cans, found the phone, saw it was home calling, answered. 'Grace?'

220

'Thank God,' her voice said, breaking a little.

'We're both safe,' he told her, his voice low, 'but I'm going to have to call you back.'

'Sam, I can't—'

He cut off the call, stuck the phone in his pocket, turned and saw Claudia in the doorway, eyes following him like a scared puppy's.

'Honey,' he said softly, 'I want you to go wait by the front door while I take a look around, but if I tell you to get out, you go straight to any neighbour's house and call the cops.'

They heard another moan.

From upstairs. No doubt.

Sam went to a drawer, opened it, winced as it creaked, saw nothing he could use, opened the next drawer down and took out a long, sharp knife.

'Oh, my God,' Claudia said. 'Sam, be careful.'

'I guess you never got to see the layout upstairs?' he asked her.

Claudia shook her head.

'OK,' he said. 'Now go to the front door.'

He waited until she was in position, then looked up the staircase.

No lights on up there.

Whoever had been doing that moaning hadn't sounded dangerous, but Sam knew better than to take anything at face value –

and just because Claudia hadn't seen Jerome Cooper since her arrival did not mean he wasn't up there waiting.

He raised his left index finger to his lips to keep her silent, gripped the knife firmly in his right hand, and began to make his way up the staircase.

The fourth stair creaked.

Sam paused, waited, moved on, hesitated again as the seventh step groaned, then made it up to the half landing. Outside, beyond the narrow window that had, from the street, seemed like a nose in the face of the house, it was raining, the external light of minimal help to him.

He heard no more moans, no other sounds of life.

And took the last few stairs.

The upstairs hallway was rectangular with four closed doors, two to the left, two to the right.

The moaning began again, softer, weaker sounding than before.

It came from the left, Sam thought, from behind the farthest door.

Moving slowly, silently, he opened the first door which led to a bathroom, pushed the door wide open, scanned to left, right, up and ahead, took two steps in to check behind the door, then moved all the way inside and pulled back the shower curtain to see into the empty bathtub.

He moved back out into the hall, silent again now, and crossed to the door opposite.

A single room with a narrow bed, double wardrobe and posters on the walls. One from a Seventies movie that Sam remembered, *The Man Who Fell to Earth*, David Bowie in profile, and facing that two more Bowie posters, one from the Ziggy Stardust era, one of the Thin White Duke.

Jerome's room, Sam supposed, swiftly opening and scanning the wardrobe, seeing a single pair of jeans, one plain white cotton T-shirt, about a dozen naked wire coat hangers and a well-trodden pair of sneakers, all suggesting that Cooper had left home altogether, not just gone to Seattle and Florida on a round-trip blackmailing excursion.

He glanced back at the posters, explored for a few seconds any possible significance in the admiration of that weak-faced, mean-eyed young man for an iconic rock-movie star.

Something jabbed at Sam's mind, something lodged in his memory.

No time to think about it now, he told himself. *Move on.*

The second room on that side of the hall was presently unoccupied, but plainly lived in, its bed a small double, neatly covered with an old-fashioned beige candlewick bedspread. Two pine wardrobes and a chest of drawers, a white-painted dressing table with a large circular mirror on a stand, a heart-shaped scented candle, a few jars and tubes of cosmetics and a box of Kleenex on the surface – and Sam knew he'd come back later for a closer look at Roxanne Lucca's belongings, but not yet.

He had the last room to check out first.

The moaner's room.

Someone either in trouble or lying in wait.

Sam stood outside the door, gripped the knife more tightly, listened.

Nothing.

He tried the handle.

The door was locked.

He crouched low, took a look through the keyhole, saw only vague grey shapes, but the acrid smell seemed stronger here, and the connection he'd made when he'd checked out his own wounds was becoming more jarring, more impossibly startling, by the second.

His call to the Sheriff's office was long overdue.

The moaning began again, louder than before.

Male, and intensely distressed.

Someone in need of help, *now*.

Sam used the knife to slide the lock open, heard and felt the blade snap.

But the door opened.

And Sam saw Frank Lucca for the first time.

224

The Epistle of Cal the Hater

In the beginning, the dressing up was just for her.

For Jewel, the white witch-bitch.

I did it to please her, too scared I'd make her mad if I refused.

Anything to stop the pain.

Then later, after I'd started getting a buzz out of the make-up and all that jazz, we kept on going – that and the other, sicko stuff too, but just between the two of us, because she said that the old guy wouldn't like it. And then, later still, after he got sick – and she wouldn't let him go to the hospital, said she was going to 'nurse' him herself – oh, man ... But after that, she started doing those 'things' to him too, and from there on everything spun way out of control. Our life inside the walls of that place was Fruitcake Alley, real Loony Tunes mixed up with a touch of Rocky Horror.

Only without any laughs.

64

'Dear God.'

Aghast was the only word for how Sam felt.

And filled with pity.

His father-in-law might have been a prize dirt-bag in his day, but he looked now as if he might have fared better serving twenty to life in Cook County Jail.

'Claudia,' Sam called from the doorway. 'Call 911, honey. We need an ambulance.'

He walked slowly back into the room.

Frank Lucca sat in a wheelchair, his bare and wasted upper body and arms restrained with bandages, his legs immobile, possibly paralyzed. There was no blanket to cover him, and no clothes except for a pair of stained and stinking off-white shorts.

He had no hair on his head, nor eyebrows. His face was greyish, his skin looking pasty in texture with deep sores on his nose and cheeks and over his lips. His eyes, bloodshot and dark, like Claudia's, were pleading.

He did not speak.

His whole body – all that Sam could see – was covered with scars and raw wounds.

Lines of them, most running vertically or diagonally over his torso, the greatest number crossing his chest.

And one of the sick, shocked feelings bombarding Sam as he took this first, long look at Grace's father, was the suspicion that when he had time to take a closer look at his own injuries, there might be similarities...

Though that was not all that was striking those chords of such horrific familiarity in his mind.

That string of thoughts kept moving on, dots continuing to connect.

The Bowie character portrayed in one of the posters in that other room was the gin-guzzling alien who fell to earth named Thomas *Jerome* Newton – and Sam remembered that because a girl he'd dated at college had been wild for Bowie; and Ziggy Stardust, he thought, had come before the alien – not that chronology counted here – but what did seem to matter right now to Sam, bewilderingly, chillingly, was that character's metallic fashion and high-heeled boots.

Like Mildred's skinny silver angel without wings.

Wearing shoes that she'd told Sam had made the guy look like he was walking 'up on the mezzanine'.

Christ almighty.

'Sir?' Sam addressed his father-in-law for the first time, unsure if the man was even

227

capable of answering.

'Sam?' Claudia called from below. 'They're coming.' Her voice wavered, as if she hadn't wanted to ask the question before. 'Is it for my father?'

'It is,' Sam called back. 'Better bring a blanket, honey.'

Another of those moans, awful in its helplessness, issued from Frank Lucca's throat, and tears leaked from his eyes.

Sam pulled a handkerchief from his own pocket, knelt down on the linoleum beside the wheelchair, and gently wiped the old man's cheeks.

Never thought this day would come.

'It's all right,' he said, softly. 'I'm Sam Becket, Grace's husband, and we're going to help you.'

Claudia came into the room, holding a blue blanket, which fell out of her hands as she saw her father, the wicked old man of her girlhood nightmares, reduced to this.

'Papa,' she said, and began to cry too.

Frank Lucca stared at her, made no further sound, his own tears stalled in his throat. He looked frozen by the sight of his long-lost daughter.

'Cut him free,' Claudia said.

'I will,' Sam said quietly and calmly, taking out his cell phone, glancing down at it, preparing its camera function, 'just as soon as I've taken some photos.'

'Evidence,' Claudia said, understanding.

'Right,' Sam said.

Two questions, first, that he knew he needed to ask.

'Who did this to you, sir?'

They waited to hear if the old man could speak.

'My wife.' Lucca's voice was faint. 'Roxanne.'

The dots went on connecting. A whole host of suspicions, all still unsustainable, still incredible, yet forming something that Sam knew was far more compelling than a hunch.

Ask the second question.

'Can you tell me, sir,' Sam said, 'if your wife ever ill-treated her son?'

Lucca's eyes seemed to burn, holding on to horrors, keeping them locked in.

And then he spoke again, a single word:

'Mostro.'

Monster.

The Epistle of Cal the Hater

So it all comes down to this. A thousand resentments building up over years like boils in your brain, erupting one at a time whenever you blow your lousy godforsaken mind. And then suddenly, there he is. This one man, this perfect target.

The prototype of everyone Jewel ever taught me to hate.

Samuel Lincoln Becket.

A whole shitload of presumption – of arrogance – in that middle name.

Middle names are important, according to Jewel, which was why she says she gave me the middle name of her favourite Bowie character. She said she didn't like his first name, Thomas, because he was the apostle who doubted Jesus, and Saint Jerome was the guy who translated the Bible into Latin. (And also, according to her, Jerome is one of Clark Kent's middle names.)

Mostly, though, Jewel was crazy about Bowie.

Mostly, she's just crazy.

65

The first thing Sam did, after he'd taken some shots of Frank Lucca's bandage bonds, then untied the poor old guy and left him to Claudia's care – was to call Grace again and put her in the picture.

'Your stepmother seems to be some piece of work,' he said. 'Though her son, I'm guessing, may have turned out even worse.'

Grace was finding it all too hard to believe.

'You can't really think Jerome could be this killer?'

'I don't have a shred of hard evidence yet,' Sam said, 'but I'm about to organize a watch on our house, just in case he decides to pay another visit.'

'Surely that's the last thing he'd do now, especially if you're right,' Grace said, then paused. 'Though if his mother's told him you and Claudia came to her house, I guess he might be angry.'

'Whatever the case,' Sam said, 'I'm not prepared to take any chances.'

His next call was to the Sheriff's office, then to Martinez back home.

'Whole lot happening here.' Martinez jumped in soon as he heard Sam's voice. 'Eddie Lopéz walked in to the office a couple of hours back.'

'He's not our guy,' Sam said. 'Eighty per cent probability, maybe more.'

He filled in his partner fast, told him that subject to a conversation perhaps now taking place between the Cook County Sheriff and Chief Hernandez, the plan was for enough departmental cooperation to allow Sam to catch the eight p.m. flight home.

'They'll take my preliminary statement, photograph my wounds—'

'You OK, man?' Martinez jumped in. 'You said *scratches* before.'

Sam had been trying to forget just how much those damned rips in his flesh were hurting. 'Nothing a little iodine won't fix.' He forced his mind back to the job. 'I found a photo of Cooper, which I'll ask Cook County to send to the Chief, so you might want to get a hold of that.'

'No problem,' Martinez said. 'How's Claudia holding up?'

'She's shaky, but up to taking care of the old man till the paramedics get here.' Arrest warrants, he went on, were being issued in Miami Beach for Jerome Cooper, and in Cook County for Roxanne Lucca.

'Nice family,' Martinez said.

'Did you find Mildred?' Sam asked.

'Not yet, not with Lopéz showing up – though at least now we can spare her the John Doe shots. Cut straight to having her ID Cooper's photo.'

'Mildred's a witness to the pick-up on Washington,' Sam said. 'We need to find her fast.'

'We're on it,' Martinez said.

Sam could hear sirens approaching in Melrose Park, allowed himself a last consideration for the gracious old lady who had put her trust in him.

'Try calling her cell phone,' he said. 'I don't want anyone scaring her.'

The Epistle of Cal the Hater

The thing Jewel liked best, I think, was the two of us getting whiter together.

If I'd been 'good', she used talcum after she'd shaved me, and then she made me help with her own whitening, make sure she'd dusted herself everywhere, and I can tell you I hated that more than anything, having to touch her private places, and even now just thinking about that makes me squirm.

When she married Frank, things got a little

easier for a while, and I guess she chose him because he owned a house, but plenty of men have plain old ordinary houses like his, so I never really figured how come Jewel could stand being with an ugly old bald wop with a hairy body. I guess the fact was, the Thin White Duke types wouldn't have looked twice at her. And of course it helped that Frank was like-minded when it came to race – especially because one of his traitor daughters had married a black Jew, so at least they had that in common. I know the old man slapped her sometimes – and maybe she liked that, and I was never sure if it made me hate him or respect him, because Christ knew I'd never had the guts to do that to Jewel.

The trouble was, Frank went out a lot to play scopone with his buddies, and the games began in the afternoons, and he never came home till the early hours, drunk as a skunk. Which wouldn't have bothered me one bit, except those were the times, while he was out, that Jewel turned into the white witch-bitch, wanting to play 'dress-up' with her boy.

Talcum not good enough anymore. She wanted to experiment with real skin-whiteners, tried everything from her good old trusty Clorox to hydrochloric acid to fucking lye, which all hurt so damned much I truly believed I was going to die.

I was still screaming one night when Frank came home and went crazy when he saw what she'd done, which was when he had his second stroke.

And after that, she did it to both of us.

I'm not sure if my mom is racist and evil.

Or just plain insane.

Like me.

'I do it because I love you so much,' she used to say sometimes when I was younger, after she'd cut me or whipped me and then poured her goddamned bleach on me and made me cry or worse.

She did love me.

I never doubted that.

66

'I only have a moment' – Claudia said to Grace on the phone, while the paramedics were tending to their father, and Sam was downstairs talking to two Cook County detectives – 'but I need to explain why I lied to you.'

'You didn't exactly lie,' Grace said. 'I assumed you were going home.'

'I as good as lied,' Claudia insisted. 'I just felt that this one time, I needed to stand up for myself, clear up my own mess.'

'You could have told me that, sis.'

'You'd never have wanted me to come here alone.'

'Maybe not,' Grace admitted.

'I wanted to come by myself to confront Papa, to make sure he and Roxanne both got to know what Jerome is really like.' Claudia lowered her voice. 'But dear God, Grace, you should just see him, see what that terrible woman has done to him – and please don't think I'm forgetting the things he did to me in the past, I'm not. But no one deserves what she did.'

Grace was silent, letting the words percolate, waiting for the fact that her father had apparently been tortured by his wife to impact on her fully, as it ought, she supposed, to impact on a daughter.

There was nothing. Nothing, at least, more than a distant kind of pity and disgust, the remote grade of feelings that stirred after reading tales of cruelty in the newspaper. Less than that. And that admission seemed to affect her more than the shocking facts about Frank, making her feel ashamed, but angry too, because it was her father's fault, not her own, that she had ceased caring about him so long ago.

She sought the right response, something that might help her sister, but only one thing sprang to the forefront of her mind, so she asked that instead.

'Have you called Daniel yet?'

'Not yet,' Claudia said. 'But soon.'

'Don't wait much longer, sis,' Grace said.

Not wanting her sister to suffer any more hurt.

Plenty of people she did still care for, still loved.

The Epistle of Cal the Hater

I knew, finally, that I had to get out or lose my mind completely.

Or maybe even die.

Which might have been better.

No escaping without money, though, and only one sure way to get it, only one talent. So I took what Jewel had taught me about dress-up and started putting it to my own advantage, with my personal homage to Ziggy, and figured I'd sell myself to the highest bidders wherever I could.

I changed my name because that's what performers do, and I did it in stages, started out just losing the first two letters of my own real name and calling myself 'Rome' – because that seemed to sit nicely with the whole orgy deal. And then I read a story about one of the Roman emperors, this crazy guy, Caligula, who screwed his sisters and had a bunch of people killed.

Which is how I came to be called Cal, and how Roxy came to be called Jewel.

Only by me, in my Epistle. She doesn't know that's how I think of her, and I know for sure that she'd hate it.

I don't like to think of what she'd do to me if she ever found out.

It was when I was reading about Caligula, and I learned that his mom's first name was Julia – which didn't suit Roxanne one bit, was too classy, too straight – but then I got to thinking how they say diamonds are the hardest substance, so I cut Julia down to Jewel, which was just perfect for her.

She doesn't know about 'Cal' either.

To my johns, I'm always Cal these days.

Tabby wasn't the first to like the name, as I recall.

I tried being plain Jerome when I went after my stepsister for money.

Which was not just for me, for the record. It was for Jewel too. I may be shit scared of my mom, but I don't always hate her, and I know what looking after that sick old bastard must have done to her, so maybe, I figured, if I made enough money, I could give her a new life too.

It isn't my fault I was brought up to hate. Not just 'those' people, but Grace and

Claudia too.

I figured it was time one of them paid for my lousy life.

Becket shouldn't have done what he did to me outside their house.

Not to Cal the Hater.

67

Mildred was in better spirits this evening.

One of her acquaintances – an occasional provider of rather fine end-of-the-day sandwiches – had dropped by to say hello earlier, and had asked Mildred if she might like to come to her coffee shop at around six for a visit, since her colleagues would be gone, which meant she'd be closing up on her own, for once.

'Tell the truth, I'd appreciate your company,' the woman had said.

Ordinarily, Mildred might have passed a dry, perhaps cynical remark, almost certainly would have done so in the privacy of her thoughts, but she liked this kind person well enough, and with the nervy mood she'd been in this past week, she thought she'd be a fool to refuse.

She was on her way there now.

68

'I really think you guys should go home,' Grace said a little after seven p.m., having bathed the baby and put him down right after another call from Chicago. 'Sam's on his way to O'Hare, and he'll be in around midnight.'

'We'll stay till he's home,' David said.

'You will not,' Grace told him, because she knew he'd been feeling really unwell, and because Saul had let slip earlier that he had a chair commission to get finished by tomorrow; besides which, she was immeasurably relieved that Sam and Claudia were both fine, but also very drained. 'You've seen the patrol cars, so I'm perfectly safe, and to be honest, I'm exhausted.'

'Which is why I think we should order in dinner,' Saul said.

'All right,' Grace gave in. 'But then you'll go home.' She laid a hand on David's craggy forehead. 'You're too warm.'

'It's June in Miami,' he said. 'I'm always warm.'

'It's cool in here,' she said. 'Saul, tell your father.'

240

'You know better than that,' Saul said.

'What do you want to eat?' David asked.

'You choose.' Grace dug out their collection of take-out menus from behind the toaster oven on the counter.

'I'm not especially hungry,' he said.

'Aha,' she said.

'So Claudia's going back home?' David changed the subject.

'As soon as Frank's settled, apparently.'

'Is he going to be OK being left that way?' asked Saul.

'I don't know,' Grace said.

She waited again for some tug within herself, some guilt or conflict pulling at her, telling her to fly to Chicago and take care of her sick old father.

There was still nothing there.

69

No problems with Sam's late check-in at O'Hare, courtesy of the Sheriff.

He moved swiftly through Terminal Three, ignoring the jolly flag-strewn concourse and most of the food court, grabbed himself a cup of black tea, swallowed down a couple of Tylenol, went through security, then headed straight to the gate, phoning home as he walked.

'I can't wait to see you,' he told Grace. 'Kiss the baby for me.'

'How about his mom?'

'Different kind of kiss,' Sam said. 'I love you, Gracie.'

His fellow passengers were already almost all on board, but he snatched another call to Martinez. 'Have you found Mildred?'

'She's been out to dinner, would you believe?' said Martinez. 'Sent me one of her texts after I called her. I'll go pick her up myself a little later.'

It was not until Sam was on the plane and seated that he understood just how bone-weary he was. His head hurt from Roxanne Lucca's crack with the heavy old gilt lamp – no prints when they'd dusted it, no big surprise – and those long, deep scratches on his chest were likely, he guessed, to be an ugly reminder for a while to come.

'We're in luck tonight,' one of the flight attendants, a nice young guy named Azam, told Sam as they waited for a go from air traffic control. 'They had a few technical problems earlier, which is why we had to switch to a 767.'

If he hadn't been so exhausted, Sam guess-ed he might have noticed sooner that his seat was a little more comfortable than the one he'd sat in on the flight out, but as the big jet began to roll around O'Hare in readiness for take-off, his tired mind was sickeningly pre-occupied with pondering the wickedness that he believed this mother had passed on to her son. Roxanne was yet to be captured, but that would happen sooner or later; Sam had enough faith in law enforcement to be sure of that and the fact that she was already as good as indicted on charges of false im-prisonment, battery, aggravated assault and probably more besides.

As for Jerome Cooper, maybe he was parti-ally to be pitied as one of Roxanne's victims, though if he had taken his cruel inheritance to monstrous new lows...

Circumstantial evidence only, to date.

Posters on a bedroom wall and the middle name of a David Bowie character – not even the same character who *seemed* to have a physical appearance in common with the young man Mildred Bleeker had described.

Wounds, on his own chest and on Frank Lucca's body, that *appeared* similar to those injuries inflicted on two men in Florida – and both sets of wounds in Illinois caused by the mother, not the son.

The stench of bleach.

If it weren't for Sam knowing that Jerome had been in the Miami area one day before the second homicide victim's body had been found – and going by Claudia's account, she'd last seen Cooper on Bainbridge Island the Monday before Sanjiv Adani's murder, which meant that the scumbag could have made it to Miami in time for that killing, too, whether he'd travelled by air or train or even by bus ... If it weren't for those timing feasibilities, all the fragile-as-hell evidence would presently be pointing to Roxanne rather than to Cooper.

But Sam would have bet his last dime.

He smiled at the businessman on his right, then looked to his left out of the window, told himself to take some mental time out.

He thought about home instead, about Grace and Joshua.

About raising a son in this scary world.

The 767 rose into the sky.

Sam was already sleeping.

70

Mildred was still feeling pretty good.

Back home again on her bench.

It was dark now, but all the fear in her seemed to have evaporated.

Nice people could do that for you, which was good to remember. To realize that even after all these years outside society, there were places inside that you could still slip into, folk who did seem to want to spend just a little time with you.

Her belly was full, the stars were coming out, the music back on Ocean Drive seemed to her just a little less raucous tonight, the ocean's waves on the kindly side too, and soon she knew she would drift off.

She remembered the call she'd had earlier from Samuel's friend, reckoned that if it had been all that important, he'd come find her here soon enough.

If he comes, he comes...

71

Cal was waiting.

He wasn't comfortable with this particular plan.

Had never done anything like this in his life.

This was bad. Worse than what he'd done to Tabby and the first guy, because when all was said and done, they'd been fools, asking for trouble and getting it.

She's asked for it too.

He supposed that was true enough. Always being there and looking at him in that judgemental way of hers, like some kind of nemesis – which was a word he'd liked ever since he'd first read it in a magazine and looked it up and learned that Nemesis had been a goddess of 'divine retribution' – and he'd never thought he'd find a use for the word, but even though it was laughable to think of *her* that way, he did.

Nemesis.

Not for much longer.

It was quiet this evening, not many people around, and Cal had prepared himself for this piece of risk-taking, knew he was going to have to be smooth as silk...

Just one couple over to the right, about twenty yards from the bench where the stinky old bird was lying in her bundles. And a man over to the left, middle-aged and paunchy, strolling peaceably along the promenade like he had all the time in the world.

Cal would have liked to kill him.

But he would not.

He'd thought long and hard about the right way to do this.

Not the same way as the others, not strangling, because that was easy enough with them walking ahead of him, not expecting trouble, expecting sex or something post-coital instead. But she was lying down.

He pictured her neck, all scrawny and old.

Wished he didn't have to go near her at all, let alone touch her.

The couple over to the right had gone, but more people were coming and going all the time, none of them coming too close to the old woman's bench because the homeless were a kind of an embarrassment to most people, and unless they wanted to poke fun or maybe slip them a buck, they kept a distance away, which was fine.

The man was still there, had stopped walking to gaze at the ocean.

He deserved to die.

If he didn't move away soon, Cal might choose to kill him after all.

The man started walking again, heading out along the sandy path on to the beach.

Cal took a look around.

Pulled on his gloves.

Took out the Leatherman knife.

Released the blade.

72

In the house on Bay Harbor Island, Grace had just beckoned Saul out of the kitchen, where David was sitting, looking at but not touching a bowl of chicken soup she'd heated up for him a few minutes ago, because he'd had no appetite either for the sushi Saul had ordered in or even for the soft boiled egg she'd offered to make him.

'I want you to take your dad home now,'

she told him. 'I'm sure he has a fever, what-ever he says.'

'I'm sure you're right,' Saul said. 'But you know Dad.'

'If we both insist, he'll just have to listen,' Grace said. 'Aside from worrying about him, I'd rather he didn't pass it on to Joshua.'

'I was thinking I could send him home in a cab,' Saul said, 'and I could stay.'

'And will your commission finish itself?' Grace asked.

'If it's me you're talking about,' David call-ed from the kitchen, 'I'm not quite finished yet.'

'We just want you to go home.' Grace step-ped into the doorway. 'Go to bed where you belong.'

'I belong here,' David said, 'until Sam gets home.'

'The last thing Sam wants is you getting sick,' Grace argued. 'The patrol cars have been coming by every ten minutes, and I have Woody, and I'll keep my phone with me the whole time in case Jerome Cooper comes busting through the window.' She saw anxiety flood into Saul's face. 'Which he will not.'

73

Mildred was dreaming about Donny.

A beautiful dream, in which they were walking hand-in-hand on South Beach, and they were both young, and her hair was shiny and falling darkly about her shoulders, and Donny let go of her hand and put his arm around her, holding her tight...

Not *his* arm.

'Don't make a sound.'

Not his voice.

'Not a sound, old woman, or I'll make you suffer long and hard.'

Mildred woke into terror.

A hand was clamped over her mouth, weight on her body, male and hard and much too heavy for her to be able to do anything to help herself.

She knew who it was.

Her angel of death, come to get her.

Help me, Donny, she called inside her head.

'You shouldn't have kept on staring at me,' he told her. 'You shouldn't have kept on *being* there.'

Mildred felt the blade slide through the light blanket and on through the layers of polyester and old wool and cotton, and if she could, she would have put up the biggest fight, because life was precious, but as slender as he'd looked, this angel was strong and she was just a weak old woman...

And maybe he was going to send her straight back to Donny.

But it hurt, Lord God, how it hurt.

Wait for me, Donny.

74

They'd woken Sam for an in-flight snack a while ago, and he'd been surprised to find that he had an appetite.

His chest still hurt, but his head felt easier, which was good news, because a concussion might have kept him off work for a day or more, and if ever there was a case that Sam Becket wanted to see through to the finish, it was this one.

Before today, he couldn't remember having felt the need to use an on-board telephone, but this 767 sported phones at every seat, and he did have the greatest urge to speak to Grace again.

The satellite was down.

Later, he thought, and went back to sleep.

75

David had caved in under their combined pressure and the undeniable fact that he felt lousy.

'I feel like I'm letting you down,' he said at the door.

'You have the flu,' Grace told him, then turned to Saul. 'Make sure he goes straight to bed, please.'

'Yes, doc,' Saul said.

'You make sure you lock up properly,' David told her.

Saul had already been right around the house with her, checking every window, making sure the doors to the deck were locked.

'And remember your phone,' David said.

'And your cell phone, too,' Saul added.

'Will you both please stop,' Grace told them. 'You're enough to make anyone a nervous wreck.'

'If you're nervous,' Saul said, 'I could—'

'Go,' she said, and opened the door.

76

A bad scene, this one.

Expedient and a whole lot less ugly than the others, but real bad.

Especially in his mind.

She'd looked no different when Cal had left her than when he'd arrived.

Just an old tramp, sleeping on her bench.

He'd rather have taken her into the dunes, done it there and left her hidden in the long wild grass, less exposed, but anything might have gone wrong along the way, and anyway, permitted or not, some people went walking in the dunes and might have stumbled on her, but the fact was, no one went around checking on sleeping vagrants to see if they were alive or dead.

Except cops, of course, on occasion.

Like Becket.

Cal had washed his knife in the ocean right after he'd done it, and then he'd tucked it back into the waistband of his shorts and pulled his T-shirt down over it.

More to do tonight.

A whole lot more.

77

The temptation to pick Joshua up out of his crib and take him to bed with her had seldom been greater.

Except chances were he'd wake later in the night, so it wouldn't be fair to disturb him now because he needed his sleep – and so did she, she supposed, so Grace suppressed the urge and instead stooped to kiss the top of his beautiful head, and left the nursery.

She went to lie down in her own, too empty, bed.

An image of Frank Lucca came into her mind.

Old and suffering, as Claudia had described him.

Telling Grace, in other words, that it was almost impossible to go on hating him now, after what he'd had to endure.

She picked up Sam's pillow, cuddled it close, breathing him in.

Pushed away the pictures of the old man.

Hung on, instead, to the fact that by the time she woke, Sam would be home.

78

Cal had been waiting again, had been for a while now.

Long enough to see the black-and-whites coming and going.

And to be as sure as he could be that Sam Becket was not home, was out working late, he guessed, hoping to catch a double killer.

Triple now.

The last time he'd come here, it had been as Jerome. Weak son of Roxanne Cooper. Her whipping boy. Less than a man.

And Samuel Becket had kicked his ass.

He should not have done that.

No way.

Now Cal, son of Jewel, was holding a burger patty in one gloved hand, stuffed full with three ground up Rest-Ezee tablets, more than enough, he'd calculated, to shut that mean, growling little dog the fuck up.

Nothing but a low gate keeping him from the back of the house – and then there was the fenced-in deck with one of those doggy doors leading right inside.

Cop daddy ought to know better.

The little runt had been yapping every

time the black-and-whites had come around, so aside from maybe getting pissed off, by now no one was going to be taking serious notice of him.

Something had put the wind up the local cops, that was for sure. The last patrol car had come around a few minutes ago. Another, ten minutes before that. Fifteen the time before. He'd made his decision to wait until right after the next circuit, then make his move.

She was alone, except for the kid. Cal was as sure of that as he could be.

Only one shadow passing across the windows since he'd been here.

Female.

Stepsister Grace.

He remembered the judgement in her eyes both times when he'd called.

Bitch.

She should only know what had happened to the last woman who'd looked at him that way – that would soon change her mind.

Just a little respect and ten thousand bucks.

He'd probably have taken five, if they'd offered it.

But Becket had kicked him.

Grace woke up again when Woody started barking, which had been happening like damned clockwork ever since David and

Saul had left, at least every fifteen minutes, and she was beginning to wonder if she could ask the cops, ever so nicely, if they'd maybe cut down their checks to twice an hour.

But with the crime rate on the islands being among the lowest in all Florida, she guessed they were glad to help. And Sam, being one of them, having asked for the patrols, they weren't likely to pay her any heed.

Anyway, she guessed she'd rather have an interrupted night than take any chances with a man like Jerome somewhere out there...

She sighed, got out of bed, went to check again that Joshua hadn't woken.

Little boy, sleeping peacefully, undisturbed and enviable.

Grace wandered over to the window, saw the brake lights of the black and white just moving away, nice and slow, and felt consoled.

Which was the general idea.

'Go to sleep,' she called softly down the staircase to Woody.

He stopped barking.

Grace went back to bed.

Sam'll be here soon.

She slept again.

Cal knew how to be quiet.

Years of practice, tiptoeing past any room

256

his mom was inhabiting.

He hadn't always managed it, what with Jewel having the ability to hear a fucking feather drop fifty feet away.

Witch-bitch.

But he'd learned how to be quiet.

79

The ringing was loud enough to wake the dead.

One phone on the bedside table, the cordless on the pillow beside her.

'Yes?' Grace said into the latter, still befuddled by sleep.

'Sweetheart, I'm sorry,' Sam's voice told her. 'I didn't mean to wake you.'

'I don't mind,' she said. 'Are you at the airport?'

'Still in the air,' he said. 'They switched planes and this one has phones, so I took advantage.'

'How much longer?'

'About an hour.'

'You must be so exhausted.' Grace felt awake now, happy to be hearing him. 'I can't wait for you to get here. If it weren't for Joshua, I'd jump in the car and come pick you up.'

'How is our beautiful boy?' Sam asked.

'Gorgeous last time I looked. All innocence, arms flung out, you know.' She stretched lazily. 'Shall I go check on him again now, tell him his daddy's on the phone?'

'Sure,' Sam said.

'Walk with me.' She got out of bed. 'Isn't this horribly expensive?'

'About five zillion bucks a second,' he said, 'but who's counting?'

She was out of their room.

Walking into the nursery.

She knew even before she was at the crib.

'Oh, my God.' The phone fell from her hand on to the floor.

'Grace?' Sam's voice sounded tinny, distant.

'Oh, dear *God.*'

'Grace, for God's sake, what's happening?'

The world felt more distant to her than Sam's voice on the floor, travelling thirty-something thousand feet up in the sky. Grace's world was spinning around her, she was down on her knees, scrabbling for the phone, and then she was up again, running like a wild, mad thing down the staircase, into the kitchen, into the den, back out into the hall, back up the stairs again in case she was wrong, crazy, in case she was the greatest fool in the world, in case she'd made a mistake.

'He's gone.'

Unreal words, ripping agonizingly out of someplace in her heart.

'Sam, he's been *taken*!'

80

The kid was in a wicker basket that Cal had bought earlier from a tourist shop in Surfside, the basket strapped to Daisy's back seat with a blue dog leash and a white plastic belt.

Quiet now, the baby, a nice enough little thing, cute too, as brown babies went, at least in the dark, and he hadn't even screamed when the stranger had picked him up out of his crib – until Cal had put his hand over his little mouth, and then he'd tried to make plenty of noise, for sure, but no one had heard – not even the dog, who was sleeping the sleep of greed, which served the little shit right. And Cal didn't know or care how much Rest-Ezee might be too much for a little dog, but the kid had settled down in the basket, and he'd read someplace that babies liked motion, that moms and dads sometimes took their yelling brats out in their cars to quieten them down, so maybe he and this kid might be lucky.

The longest ride of his life had barely begun, he knew that. He'd stayed on Collins, because though it seemed endless on the tandem, and his legs were already hurting from pumping the pedals, and his back and shoulders were still sore from taking care of Tabby, it was still straighter and easier than taking back roads. And he'd taken a gamble on no one having seen him – and face it, no one had, because otherwise they'd have been on him already, wouldn't they, black-and-whites and maybe unmarked cars cutting him off and slamming him and Daisy to a halt. But there weren't any cop cars and not a whole lot of life of any kind out here to-night, so he was planning on staying on Collins until 63rd, and then he'd be on Alton, and at least then he'd feel like he was getting someplace.

His biggest problem right now, aside from the pain, was having too much time to think about what he was doing.

About what he'd done earlier that evening.

Because all this was – there was no denying it – premeditated. Which meant that Cal knew now, without any fragments of doubt to console him, that he had become an evil man.

He began to feel an urge to weep as he cycled through the warm night.

When he was done with this, he would have to punish himself again, *deeper* wounds this time, deeper than any he'd ever inflicted on himself or anyone else.

When he was done with this.

When he was *done*.

81

Screaming in his head.

Grace's and his own.

And all Sam could do was make lousy phone calls from the sky.

His hands were shaking, and his voice, too, and his body, inside and out.

Trying to stay in control, only just making it.

Bay Harbor PD first, because Joshua had been taken in their jurisdiction, and this had to be done right, and he knew they would do that, knew they would have done that for any child, let alone the baby son of one of their own. They would bring in FDLE and the Child Abduction Response Team and – if Jerome Cooper acted on previous *known* form and got in touch, demanding a ransom – then the FBI would come in, too. And if Sam heard so much as a flicker of hesitation in the voice of whoever he spoke to, he would make all those calls himself, haul every last special agent and investigator and

261

detective out of their beds and into Miami Beach, but for now, at least, he was going to do it by the book.

And one of the things he wished to Christ he could do right now was to wipe every damnable learned statistic from his own policeman's mind, because the facts were that forty-four per cent of abducted children were killed within the first hour of being taken, seventy-four per cent within three hours, ninety-one within twenty-four hours, rising to ninety-nine per cent in seven days.

Screaming in his head.

The call to Bay Harbor had been made – and Sam had heard no hesitation, no fumbling, just clear and positive help – and so now he was calling Martinez, because jurisdiction and correctness aside, Alejandro Martinez was his trusted friend and a damned fine detective, and if there was just one extra step that could be taken, Martinez would go for it.

Another thirty minutes at least in the air.

The number was ringing.

Don't be scared, Joshua, he told his sweet baby boy. *Daddy's coming.*

Martinez picked up his cell phone.

His voice sounded bad, like he already knew.

'I got bad news,' he said, right off. 'Someone – I guess Cooper – got to Mildred.'

Another fracture in Sam's breaking heart. 'Al, I got worse news,' he told his friend.

82

In a line of passengers just debarked from the seven thirty out of Chicago O'Hare, a tall, lean, blonde woman in a white trouser suit walked with the rest through Concourse D at Miami International, passing the desperadoes in the smoking room.

It was a long walk, even bypassing the baggage claim, and all the while she was still half expecting a uniform to step out ahead of her, as she'd anticipated earlier that evening at O'Hare. But either, she supposed, Becket and Claudia were still trussed up, or maybe she'd hit him harder than she'd thought; or maybe her crimes just didn't merit urgent messages to airports the way they seemed to on TV, or maybe the police in Melrose Park or Cook County were just plain sloppy.

It had been sloppy of her, too, to have paid for her ticket with her MasterCard, but even if she'd had enough cash to pay with, that might have attracted more immediate attention, and then after she'd used the card anyway, she'd figured she might as well use it again to take money out of an ATM. All of which meant that they would be tracing her to Miami by morning at the latest, but she'd just have to worry about that then.

After she'd found Jerome.

She might never have troubled to track him down again, let alone gone to this much trouble to save his miserable hide if Claudia had not come back to Melrose Park just to tell her and Frank about his botched blackmail attempts.

As well for his mother to know what Jerome had been up to.

High time she found him and put a stop to his nonsense before he got himself into real trouble, got himself put back in the slammer.

Everyone had their purpose, even her pathetic older stepdaughter.

Frank had always said she was the weaker of the two sisters.

Though at least Claudia had made a decent marriage, unlike the other one.

She could certainly understand Jerome's loathing of Sam Becket. Though it seemed, luckily, that the black Jew wasn't that much of a cop if he hadn't read Jerome his goddamned rights as soon as he'd stuck his idiot nose through his front door.

But if only her son had possessed the brains of a fucking flea, *she* wouldn't have been forced into taking her stepdaughter prisoner or assaulting a goddamned police detective, not to mention leaving her own

home and flying halfway across the country.
On the run, at her time of life.

Jesus, but he had a lot to answer for.

83

Grace was in meltdown. Every last cell of her being was shrieking to be out there trying to find her son, even if meant ransacking every house or apartment or store, every warehouse or garage or hotel room in Miami – in Florida – in the whole *country*...

'They could be anywhere,' she told the men and women, uniformed and plain-clothed, who had invaded and all but taken over her house. She paced as she spoke, moving in and out of the kitchen, walking to and fro in the small hallway, her eyes wide with desperation, her voice uncharacteristically loud and shrill, because she needed them to listen to her, to understand, to be *out* there, not in here, doing nothing but standing around. 'We need road blocks, we need—'

'We're doing everything we can, Mrs Beck-et,' one of the female officers told her, a stranger in a blue trouser suit with short fair hair and pale eyes.

'You are *not*,' Grace told her back, with

venom, 'because if you were, then my baby would be back here with me.'

More people came into the house and she raked each one with her eyes, but they did not have Joshua in their arms, which made them worse than *useless* to her. And the only useful thing anyone seemed to have done was to take poor doped Woody to an emergency veterinarian, and she felt so bad for him, but at least he was now being cared for, while her son was not, her son was with an evil man somewhere out there.

'You have to let me go look for him,' she told them.

'Plenty of people doing just that, ma'am,' a man told her gently.

She didn't recognize him, but he was in a blue Bay Harbor uniform, and deep down Grace knew very well that he was in no way to blame, but right then she wanted to shove him aside or even pound his kind, earnest face with her fists, to scream at him.

Except, of course, he was *not* to blame, any more than the patrol officers who had not been outside the house at precisely those moments when Jerome Cooper had put drugged meat through the doggy door. And somewhere in the recesses of her torn-up mind, she supposed that *they* were very much to blame for that, she and Sam, most *especially* Sam, because if anyone knew better...

She told herself to stop that.

Because there was only one person really to blame.

Why had she been so *stubborn*, insisting on being left alone? Why had she not let Saul stay with her, as he'd suggested over and over? Why had she not given in to her impulse to bring Joshua into bed with her? Why hadn't she made certain she spent every single second in the same room as her innocent boy until Sam was back and Cooper safely under arrest?

She'd convinced herself that there was no real danger, that Jerome could not possibly be the double killer, that whether he was or not, he would not come back here, where it was so obvious that he would be placed under arrest.

But Sam had figured differently. Sam – who knew more than she did about the ways that evil worked and connived – had arranged the patrol, had called his father and brother because he'd *known* there might be danger.

And she had thought she knew better.

More people came through the front door – David and Saul back again.

'Gracie,' David said.

She collapsed into his familiar, kindly arms, weeping, then quickly pulled away again, wiped fiercely at her eyes. 'You're sick. You shouldn't be here.' She turned on Saul.

267

'You should have known better.'

'Stop that,' David told her. 'Is there no news?'

Grace shook her head, saw how pale Saul was, felt another pang of guilt, tossed it quickly aside for more important things. 'They won't let me go look for him.'

'They're right,' David said. 'You need to be here.'

'I need to be out there, finding our son.'

'You need to be here,' Saul said, 'in case Cooper calls.'

She knew that he meant for a ransom, because of what had happened the last time Jerome had come here – and for a moment, Grace felt fresh fury sear her insides at Claudia for bringing this to them.

'He won't call,' she said, swallowing down the anger.

'You don't know that,' David said.

'Anyone can answer the phone,' Grace said. 'I want to be with Joshua.'

It rang.

Everyone froze.

Grace didn't wait to be told, moved suddenly, snatched up the phone on the kitchen wall, close to the door. 'Yes?'

'Gracie, it's me,' Sam said. 'I'm on the ground, coming straight home.'

'Don't come home,' she said. 'You need to look for Joshua.'

'Better people than me doing that already,'

268

he told her, sounding halfway steady, 'and I'm going to be out there with them soon as I can, but right now I'm coming home to you.'

Grace saw and felt everyone on the first floor watching her, listening, and she turned her back on them as best she could, stepped into the corner of the kitchen closest to Joshua's playpen, wishing she could melt through the wall, escape them all, escape her own shame.

'Sam, I'm so sorry,' she said.

'Are you crazy?' he said. 'What do you have to be sorry for?'

'I let him take our son,' she said.

84

June 12

Ten minutes into Thursday, huddled below on *Baby*, Cal heard the trill of his cell phone.

He knew without looking that it was her, because no one else ever called.

He shrivelled at the thought of hearing Jewel's voice.

Yet in another way he longed to talk to her. Pitiful.

'Hello, Mother.'

'What the fuck have you been doing, Jerome?' asked Roxanne Lucca.

Cal felt his blood turn to ice, because she truly *was* a witch, otherwise how would she know? And then that overwhelming need descended on him, the need for confession, the need for her *help*, because what he'd done was way too much for him, he realized that now. The thing was, he didn't know what to do next, and up until now he'd thought he mightn't care if he got caught, but that wasn't true, not at *all*, because the things he'd done were so terrible, and now he was more scared of what they'd do to him on Death Row and after than he was of Jewel and her brand of punishment.

'Who the fuck,' she went on, 'is stupid enough to blackmail a cop's family?'

Which meant she didn't know the half of it.

'I need you, Mom,' he said, already quaking.

The words were out of his mouth before he could stop them, and he wasn't sure that he did need her, knowing she was poison, knowing she was the root of all his evil, but he'd said it now and there was no pulling it back, no magic rewind.

'Tell me where you are,' she said, 'and I'll come to you.'

Don't tell her.

'I'm in Miami,' he told her.

'Me too,' Roxanne said. 'Now tell me the fuck *where*?'

She was still at the goddamned airport, waiting in line in the hot, humid night air for a cab.

Going to see her idiot son.

On the fucking run.

85

Sam was back home on the island.

Two crazed parents now under one roof.

Outside, the stars and moon had disappeared again behind the dark weight of another brewing June storm, but almost everyone in the semi-circle of their street was up and about now; startled, shocked, well-meaning people checking their back yards and garages, allowing the police to move in and out of their houses.

Sam went with Grace out on to their deck, trying not to let her realize that he was scanning the dark water out back.

'Do you think I haven't done that fifty times already?' Grace said tightly.

They both turned, came close together, clung on for a moment, then stepped apart again.

'If anything happens—'

'Hush.' Sam raised two fingers, held them against her lips.

Grace stared into his eyes, waited till his hand dropped away.

'If anything bad has happened to Joshua,' she went on – 'worse than *this*, I won't blame you if you kill me.'

'You fell asleep,' Sam said. 'You thought he was OK and you fell asleep.'

'How could I do that?' Grace asked, bewildered.

'You woke and checked on him.' Sam knew he sounded more rational than he felt, knew he had to do this for her. 'Like the patrol checked on the house, and he still came in.' He shook his head. 'Shall we kill those officers too?'

'They're not his mother.'

'I'm his father,' Sam said. 'I installed that damned door for the dog.' His first lost son, Sampson, came into his mind as he had many times since he'd heard Grace's first cry, and he gritted his teeth and sent him away again. 'I'm his daddy,' he said, 'I wasn't here.'

'Because of my family,' Grace said.

Sam took hold of her hands, gripped them tightly, felt how cold she was. 'Shall we go on with this, go on punishing ourselves? Or shall we go and help get our son back home?'

'You already lost one son.' She couldn't seem to stop.

'Which is why I'm not going to lose another,' Sam said.

'You trusted me with Joshua.'

His grip was tighter than ever, his eyes darker, fiercer.

'And I always will,' he said.

86

It was almost one thirty when Roxanne reached Flamingo Marina.

Another five minutes before she found the boat.

She saw him on board, hunched down at the dock side, waiting for her.

He stood up.

'Well blow me down,' she said. 'Captain Cooper.'

'Hello, Mother,' Cal said, and put out a hand to help her aboard.

'Very gallant,' Roxanne said. 'My son, the failed blackmailer.'

And then she slapped him, as hard as she could, across the face.

'How do you know about that?' Cal's eyes and cheeks were stinging, but he didn't care, it was what he wanted. 'How did you know I was in Miami?'

'Your stepsister Claudia told me,' Roxanne

said. 'Paid me a visit to complain about you. Like that's what I needed in my miserable life.'

'But that's part of why I was doing it,' he said. 'For you. So you could leave the old man, come away with me.'

'Bullshit,' Roxanne said. 'You're almost pissing yourself now, you're so scared of me.'

'I think,' Cal said slowly, 'I'm more scared of me.'

Even in the dark, his mother's eyes were like knives.

'What the fuck else have you done?'

'You have to help me,' Cal said.

A night heron circled overhead and called.

'I'm your mother,' Roxanne said. 'Now tell me.'

The bird's raucous cry came again, was buried beneath a rumble of thunder.

'Come below,' Cal said. 'And I will.'

87

Martinez arrived at the house, his face strained with a mixture of dismay and staunch determination to keep it together.

He came out back with Sam on to the deck while Grace was upstairs, helping Saul persuade David to rest a while in Cathy's room.

No rain was falling yet, but the sky flashed and flickered with an almost phosphorescent shimmer and thunder rolled around somewhere over to the east.

'Biggest manhunt on the Beach since Cunanan,' Martinez said.

Which most law enforcement officers considered a failed manhunt because Gianni Versace's killer had committed suicide before he could be arrested. Which both Sam and Martinez felt, in their souls, Jerome Cooper was more than welcome to successfully attempt.

After they had Joshua safely back home.

Martinez had only one piece of half-good news.

'Mildred's in Miami General.'

'I thought you said he killed her,' Sam said.

'Not quite.'

Sam had thought his hate quota for Jerome all maxed out.

'What did he do to her?'

'Stabbed her,' Martinez said. 'On her bench sometime last evening.' He paused. 'They don't know yet if she's going to make it.'

Sam took another moment to absorb that and to regroup.

'So what are we doing hanging around here?' he said.

'You have to stay here,' Martinez told him.

'Not while my son is out there with a goddamned killer.'

'Grace needs you, man.'

'What Grace needs,' Sam said, 'is for me to bring Joshua home.'

88

Cal could see that it was a lot for any mother to take in.

Even Jewel.

The fact that her son was a multiple murderer.

And now a kidnapper, too.

Of the baby son of a policeman.

'Let me get this straight,' she said. 'You did this for money?'

Cal saw incredulity and something else, something darker, richer, that made his insides quake.

'Not for money,' he said. 'Not this. For payback.'

They were below now on *Baby*, and he wished he could at least sit down, but she was still standing, stooping a little too, since she was as tall as he was. And maybe not quite as physically strong, but with a viciousness deep within her soul that he doubted he could ever really beat.

Not that he'd ever tried.

'Where is the baby?' Roxanne asked.

'If I tell you,' Cal said, 'you have to promise—'

She backhanded him, a silver ring on her right hand cutting his nose.

'What did you do with that goddamned *baby*?'

'What do you think I did?' he said.

Still standing, not cowering, and this was something new, at least, something left to be proud of, after all.

'You killed a baby?'

Not just knives in her eyes now, daggers.

'You killed *their* baby?'

And not the same height as him, after all, *taller*.

And Cal knew what was coming now.

'Lie down,' his mother said.

'No,' he said.

'Do it,' she told him.

And she shoved him with both hands, palms out towards him, so hard that he struck the door to the head and *Baby* rocked.

'*Do* it,' Jewel-the-white-witch-bitch ordered him.

And Cal had believed that was what he wanted, her punishment, to be flayed, for his flesh to be ripped and burned.

He knew different now.

And the knife was still in his waistband under his T-shirt.

'Lie the fuck *down*, imbecile,' his mother screamed at him.

'*You* lie the fuck down,' Cal the Hater told her.

And pulled out the knife.

And stuck it through her ribcage and into her heart.

89

Martinez had already been to the office, had worked some Adobe magic to turn Cooper's photograph into a version that transformed him into the probable silver dude of Mildred's description. Hard evidence and a real *lead* on the sonofabitch's possible whereabouts were what they most needed to consolidate the manhunt – to which end he and Sam were now in his Chevy heading to Hot-Hot-Hot and Menagerie, the two clubs most likely to have been where Cooper had picked up the man Mildred had seen him with. Because maybe their killer was a regular, and maybe someone *knew* him, and maybe, just *maybe*, this kind of plain, slogging detective work might get them someplace.

Helpful people at the first club, but not so much as a whisker of recognition.

Menagerie was winding down, no one

exactly unfriendly, but most people too drunk or stoned or just too tired to tax their brains. The bartender *not* the guy who would have been on duty in the early hours of yesterday morning.

It took time to rustle up the manager to find the off-duty bartender's address.

'But you won't find him there,' the guy told them. 'He's on vacation, told me he was going home for two hours' sleep, then heading out to the airport.'

'Where'd he go?' asked Martinez.

Sam was already on his way out the door, knowing a dead-end when he saw one, not willing to waste one more minute.

Black-and-whites were everywhere, cruising slowly, Miami Beach's finest all looking for Cooper, for any thin young guy, drab or silver, on foot, in a car, on a bus or on a tandem, all galvanized by their most urgent and earnest desire to find Joshua Becket alive and well.

'Where next?' asked his partner, joining him on the sidewalk.

The first splashes of rain began to mark the concrete, striking the car roof with enough clatter to promise heavier stuff to come.

Sam's brain felt like it was dying, but he willed it to kick-start.

Enough cops out here already, aimlessly searching.

Direction still what they needed.

'Back to Satin.' The nightclub where Adani's boyfriend had worked. 'Maybe our guy was a regular there.'

'Then let's go wake up Lopéz,' Martinez said, getting back in the car. 'Show him the photos, just in case.'

90

Three in the morning, and nothing left here in Flamingo Marina for Cal.

Except horror.

Nothing for him any other place either. Not now that he had committed the worst crime in the world.

Matricide.

He'd probably use that word in the Epistle some day, he thought, liking the sound of it inside his head, but he'd left his writings in the dump in the alleyway, and there could be no going back there ever again.

Cal supposed that ultimately the cops – and maybe their shrinks too, maybe even some FBI profiler – would pore over his words, and that was fine with him. He had, he guessed, always half wanted the Epistle to be read, his writing analysed, maybe even admired.

Maybe one day, if he survived this, he'd

280

start over, write some more.

But for now, all he could do was sit on top of the steps on *Baby*, raindrops falling on his sinful head, trying not to think about his dead mother down below.

Wondering which would be worse.

Going to hell right off, or being sent there via a fucking lethal injection for being a multiple killer.

And don't forget the baby.

Cop's baby.

'Imbecile,' Jewel had called him.

Not altogether wrong.

He hadn't shown her the kid, had balked at that.

Hell, he figured, was maybe the one thing stopping him from killing himself right away.

Though maybe he ought to at least start planning how to do it.

Not quite yet though.

Things to do.

91

There were still police officers in the Beckets' kitchen, ready to monitor and trace phone calls. Mary Cutter was with them now, Sam's colleague sent over by Alvarez to help support Joshua's mom, but for the time being Cutter was feeling redundant and useless.

Grace was alone, huddled on the couch in the den, the phone beside her.

Joshua's favourite little blue stuffed bear was clutched in her right hand, close to her face, up against her nose, her son's scent on it, so that if she shut her eyes...

She'd been rocking herself, back and forth, back and forth.

Just enough self-control left to stop that when people came in to check on her, to offer her cups of tea, shoulders to cry on, a listening ear, something to eat.

'No, thank you,' she'd say, then ask them to shut the door.

As soon as they'd gone, she started rocking again.

Not that it comforted her, yet she felt compelled to do it.

The storm seemed to be making it even worse, magnifying her fears with each successive thunder roll, her baby out there in *that*, with a man whose appearance had been utterly ordinary, but who had turned out to be worse than a blackmailer or even a kidnapper, who was almost certainly a killer, a *beast*...

Claudia had called a while ago, but Grace had asked Saul to speak to her.

She just couldn't do that herself.

Not that she blamed Claudia for what had

happened.

She mustn't do that, must not...

She just couldn't speak to her or anyone else, neither Claudia nor Mary Cutter nor Cathy, who would probably call from California in the morning and, who Grace was determined would remain in blissful ignorance until it was over.

Until Sam came home with Joshua.

92

Satin was closed, and Eddie Lopéz was not home.

'No point trying to hunt him down tonight,' Sam said.

They went to Lummus Park, to Mildred's home, now a crime scene.

Her bench was gone, had been removed from its base and taken to the ME's office, the area around cordoned off, two officers keeping watch.

Nothing here to help them find Joshua.

No word, either, on the whereabouts of Roxanne Lucca.

'You need to go home,' Martinez told Sam.

'Not yet,' Sam said.

Despair felt like ice-cold iron squeezing his heart.

'We got no place to look,' his friend said.

'We need to look everywhere,' Sam said.

'Plenty of people doing that already,' Martinez said. 'You gotta go home, man. You need to be with Grace.'

'Boats,' said Sam.

Two bodies, two boats. Stood to reason.

'We should be searching *boats*,' he said.

'All kinds of people on that too,' Martinez said patiently, though he knew he'd told Sam that earlier. 'Every marina, every anchorage, every mooring. It's going to take time.'

Sam wanted to go out and personally rip apart every last boat in Florida.

Frustration rose like sickness in his chest.

'One more thing before I do go home,' he said.

He wanted to see Mildred.

93

Cal woke with a jolt a little after four.

Still sitting on top of the steps on *Baby*.

Human remains below.

The storm was closer than it had been, rain falling steadily, no deluge yet; the sounds the drops made as they tumbled on to the water in the quiet marina were almost comforting, the cruiser rocking, bumping against...

Sirens.

In the distance.

Not for me.

Not yet.

Things to do.

Miles to go before I sleep.

He thought that came from a poem, one he'd come across a long time ago during one of his reading periods when he'd devoured poems, newspapers, Bible stories, *Playboy*, cereal packs, Jewel's *National Enquirer* and *Readers Digest*, TV Guides, whatever was there...

He stood up and cracked his head on the door frame.

'Fuck,' he said.

Time to sharpen up.

Things to do.

94

Mildred was in the Critical Care Unit, the same place in which Sam had spent a whole lot of hours last year.

A nurse told him that Mildred was holding her own.

She looked very different in the bed, in the hospital gown. So much smaller without her layers yet, despite her fragility, somehow not really as diminished as she might have been.

Strong lady, God willing.

Sam wondered how she would react, if she made it through, to being in this place, to being inside, being cared for. He remembered her telling him that since Donny's death she had not been able to endure walls around her.

The people within these walls were kindly, were doing their best to save her life, but Sam didn't know if Mildred would be able to feel gratitude or any measure of relief, or if she might be frustrated or even angry at being penned in.

He hoped she wouldn't be too afraid.

He hoped that she would, above all, have the will to go on living.

'It's Samuel,' he told her, squeezing her right hand gently. 'You be strong.'

The machines beeped softly, continued on their way.

'I got a bottle of Concord Grape with your name on it, Mildred,' he said, 'just waiting for you to get out of here.'

Now he wanted to weep.

So he got the hell out before he started.

95

David came downstairs at ten to five.

Grace heard him, stopped rocking before the door opened.

'You should be sleeping,' she told him.

Knowing suddenly, despite that, that he was one person to whom she could bear to speak.

'I slept,' he said.

'I don't suppose,' Grace said, 'you'd consider going home to bed.'

'You don't suppose right,' he said.

She patted the couch. 'Join me?'

'I may be infectious,' David said.

A thousand instant thoughts flew like sharp-billed birds through Grace's mind – all coming down to one that pecked right into her heart. The very worst thought. That she might never again have to worry about Joshua catching the flu or any other illness.

'Sit with me,' she said. 'Please.'

Saul appeared in the doorway.

'You look worse than I do, son,' his father told him.

'Mind if I join you guys?' Saul asked.

A second person she didn't mind.

'Come,' Grace said.

The three of them sat in a line on the couch, not speaking much, not huddling together, just their arms touching lightly.

Small comfort, for a very little while.

96

In the darkness, Cal was taking *Baby* out of the marina.

Cal the Sailor again.

Liberating one more dinghy as he left Flamingo – easy as blinking, two slices with his knife and more than enough line left to lash her to *Baby's* cleat.

Cleat-clit.

Good job.

The police activity inland was growing ever more audible, plenty more sirens, and if he'd gone ashore he imagined he'd have seen black-and-whites moving back and forth, spreading through Miami Beach and the city and beyond, maybe coming out to the marinas, large and small, all hands out there now, all looking for the cop's kid and for *him*...

He was not going ashore, not for a long while, maybe never.

Heading north.

The rain was getting heavier, though the storm was not yet quite overhead, but still it was angry sounding, thunder and lightning coming in great clusters all around, rumbles and deeper, more violent claps, the flashes like ten thousand paparazzi cameras lighting up heaven...

Not going there, for sure.

Cal took *Baby* carefully through the markers in the dark waters, steering her around Belle Island and on through the channel and past the Sunset Islands, trying to keep to just under the prescribed thirty miles an hour, because no *way* was he going to risk attracting unnecessary attention.

Maybe he'd just keep on going until he ran out of fuel.

Maybe he'd head out through Haulover Cut right out to sea, then drift around in that vast old Atlantic bathtub and starve to death.

Except they wouldn't let him do that.

Nothing so easy.

He passed beneath the east bridge of the Julia Tuttle Causeway again, just the way he had with Tabby on board, though the waters were choppier tonight, and he saw that another boat was coming his way through the Moley Channel, and his insides lurched with *Baby*'s motion and clenched up with fear at the same time, because maybe this was it, maybe they were coming for him...

Not the Coast Guard, nor the cops, not yet at least. Just an old fishing boat chugging its way home or out for an early start, its owner minding his own business, and soon enough *Baby* was passing unhindered under 79th, making the curve around Normandy Isle. He'd gotten to know these waters pretty well, one way or another, and Cal thought he might miss them after he was gone, figured it might have been fun to spend innocent, carefree time around here, taking his little cruiser out for long days around the Bay and beyond, maybe doing a little fishing of his own or even learning to dive, and he'd seen on his chart that there were a bunch of sunken ships right off Miami Beach, even a goddamned 727 airplane which had broken in half after some tropical storm; though most of the wrecks, Cal knew, had been deliberately submerged to make artificial reefs, which to his way of thinking made it a whole lot less fun than if they'd sunk or crashed and burned by accident...

Concentrate, he told himself, passing under the last causeway before Haulover, cutting his speed further, making sure he stuck between the right markers, because he was almost there now, and in the Cut itself the water was even more turbulent than it had been last night, giving *Baby* a pounding, but she was doing great, she was fine, and he *loved* her for taking such good care of him, loved her more, he thought, feeling his heart seem to expand, than he'd ever loved any human, even Jewel.

And then he was through the worst of it, and back out in the great, free ocean, and he said the word out loud:

'Free.'

Then said it again, louder still, letting the vowels stretch into the night air.

'Freee...'

And then he cut the engine.

Not ready to weigh anchor, not yet.

He felt better out here, up in the open salty air with the wild, flashing sky above, and he guessed now that there was no God after all, because now would surely have been the moment for Him to strike him down with a thunderbolt, maybe turn *Baby* into a god-damned floating Old Sparky – though maybe He was just biding His time, and if it did happen, if Cal had time to register, to feel, maybe he'd be nothing much more than grateful. But for now, it was just the ocean and the flaring skies keeping the rest of it at bay for a little while longer, making believe it was just him and *Baby* and their new dink on the start of a voyage. And he had a little cash now, because he'd taken over a hundred bucks from Jewel's wallet, and her cell phone, too, so if he wanted to...

He doubted he was going to have much use for the cash.

Neither in jail nor in hell.

But he was going to use her phone, rather than his own.

Just as soon as he felt strong enough.

No one to help him now, no one left in the whole miserable fucking world.

Which was all *their* fault.

Becket's mostly.

Though not the baby's, poor little kid.

At least Cal thought he'd seemed to enjoy the tandem ride.

No more rides on Daisy for Cal.

God, he was tired now, would have liked to sleep again.

The last of the Rest-Ezee had gone into the kid, because he couldn't risk him bawling his little lungs out back in the marina.

Not a peep out of him since then.

Just a few more things Cal had to do before he made his call.

Miles to go.

Going nowhere.

97

The phone rang just as Sam came through the front door.

'I'll get it!' Grace cried out, already in the hallway because she'd heard the Chevy pull up, had known it was Martinez's car.

Sam's arms were empty.

She turned, pushed past David and Saul back into the den, snatched up the phone. 'Yes?'

'I'm sorry,' a male voice said.

She knew him right away.

'Jerome,' Grace said, and began to shake.

Sam, right behind her, signalled to her to keep Cooper talking, then moved silently out of the room and into the kitchen to pick up the cordless extension, while two officers at the table, ready and calm, went for a trace.

'I didn't plan on taking the baby,' Jerome told Grace. 'Not at—'

'Where is he?' Grace's voice was high and sharp. 'What have you—?'

'If you want him back,' Jerome said, 'shut up.'

'All right,' Grace said.

Her mind felt split in a kind of bifocal concentration, most of it riveted by Cooper, waiting for him to speak again, wanting to reach through the phone and physically drag the words, the *truth*, out of his throat; but another portion of her brain free enough to be aware of the goings on in the house as Martinez came in, took in the situation, slipped silently into the kitchen with the others.

'Remember baby Moses?' said Jerome Cooper.

293

Bulrushes flew into Grace's mind – then boats bearing bodies.

'You put him in a boat,' she said.

'I said shut up,' Jerome told her, and the connection crackled.

'I'm sorry,' Grace said, and stopped breathing.

'Closer than you think,' Jerome said.

And ended the call.

Grace gave a cry, threw the phone on to the couch and pushed past uniforms into the kitchen, saw instantly from Sam's expression that it had been too short.

'Not enough time,' one of the officers at the table confirmed.

'In a boat,' Sam said, and grasped Grace's left hand. 'Joshua's in a boat.'

'He didn't say that, I did.' Grace pulled her hand free. 'He said "Remember baby Moses".'

'He's in a boat,' Sam said with grim and absolute certainty.

'The line was bad,' Grace said. 'There was interference.'

'The storm,' Sam said.

Still rolling around out there.

'Closer than you think.'

'Miami-Dade and the Coast Guard can get their choppers up at dawn,' Martinez said.

'Someone get me a boat,' Sam said. 'Now.'

'It's too dark,' Mary Cutter said.

'You think I'm waiting for light?' Sam said.

'I'm not sure you have a choice, son,' David said from out in the hallway. 'With the storm and—'

'Drew Miller has a powerboat,' Grace broke in.

Their neighbour, three houses along.

Sam was already halfway to the front door. Grace right behind him.

He turned to hug her.

'Don't bother,' Grace told him. 'I'm coming with you.'

98

Cal was too afraid to look at the baby again.

It had been so still and silent when he'd opened the hatch and taken the basket out of the storage space beneath, such a reproachful looking thing that he'd had to tear his eyes away from it.

He supposed he ought to check its pulse.

Not *it*. He. *His* pulse.

If he still had one.

Cal wasn't sure how much a baby that age could withstand. He knew it had survived being removed from its crib, knew it had taken pretty well to the long cycle ride – well enough to have still been alive, anyway – but then it had been given crushed up Rest-Ezee and put down under the floor, and he'd thought about air, had figured it would be able to breathe, but he didn't know that for sure, didn't know if there'd been *enough* air getting through to its little lungs...

'Where is the baby?' Jewel had asked him.

He would have told her if she'd only given him a chance.

But she'd backhanded him instead.

'I didn't mean it,' Cal said now.

And chanced another swift glance at the kid.

Too still.

Cal looked away again.

'I'm sorry,' he said. 'Real sorry.'

99

Their neighbour's boat was named *Windswept*.

Three of them were on board, all wearing lifejackets and the nearest to boating shoes in all their sizes that they'd been able to dig up in their own and Drew Miller's wardrobes. Martinez had been as insistent as Grace on coming along. An extra pair of eyes, he'd said, and no one had argued with him, though when Miller had offered to take them out, he had been thanked but refused, because no way was Sam going to risk harm coming to a civilian.

'Any damage,' Sam had told him, 'we'll take care of it.'

'Do you think I give a damn?' Miller had said. 'Just find your son.'

A swift rush of something like love had made Sam hug the guy, and then Miller had shown them the controls, helped them untie the lines and then walked away.

'Riley just called,' Martinez told Sam as they began to move. 'Wants you to know Alvarez is riding with her, and a lot of our people are heading out on boats too.' His smile was grim. 'Sounds like Dunkirk.'

'That's great,' Sam said.

Time to thank them all later.

'Careful,' Grace told him now.

Neither of them were sailors, though she had, years ago, planned to buy a small boat of her own some day, that particular ambition sunk by a terrifying experience she'd never been able to entirely forget.

Lord knew she'd go through worse than that to get Joshua safely back.

'You gotta stay between the markers,' Martinez said. 'I don't know much, but I know it's shallow and if we hit bottom, we're not going anyplace.'

'You guys just watch the water,' Sam told them.

Neither Grace nor Martinez needing the

reminder.

The rainpower increased, became a Florida deluge, making visibility harder and their concentration even greater, and the sporadic lightning flashes flooding the sky turned the dark waters to monochrome and silver, granting them seconds at a time to scan the choppy surface around the powerboat. They had two flashlights and a small searchlight given to them by one of the patrol units, and a pair of binoculars loaned them by Drew Miller, but all the inadequate fragments of light brought them more illusions than clarity; and as Sam moved the *Windswept* cautiously into Indian Creek, each time Grace saw so much as the glint of a ripple, her heart leapt crazily, but then she looked more closely and there was nothing to see but white froth and black water.

Closer than you think, Cooper had said.

Though perhaps that had been mind games, maybe even the ultimate perverse desire to lure them out here, and maybe Joshua was on land after all.

But Grace didn't believe that.

'Moses was found in a river,' she said.

'Miami River, you think?' Martinez said.

'Just watch the water,' Sam told them.

100

Cal had finished making all his preparations.

The torrential rains had slowed, the big drops falling more steadily again, and it seemed to him now that the sky was not quite as dark as it had been just a short while ago.

First glimmer of dawn way ahead on the horizon.

Straight on till morning.

Jewel had taken him to see *Peter Pan* once upon a time, back home in Peoria, before they'd moved upstate in search of some kind of better life, and she'd been strange even in those early days, but Chicago had made her worse.

He remembered how much he'd enjoyed the Disney movie, remembered feeling that Jewel had seemed almost like a real mom that afternoon.

Hadn't even lasted till evening, as he recalled.

'Hey, mom,' he said to her now.

Not sure if he was talking to the body down below or something further away.

No heaven for Jewel, that was for sure.

The sudden realization that *she* might be waiting for him down in hell added a whole new dimension to what he'd already been feeling.

Forget fear.

That was real terror.

101

There was nothing to be seen in the narrow channels leading around La Gorce Island, but a whole lot of lights and activity way up ahead around the JFK Causeway and beyond in Biscayne Bay.

'Our people out that way.' Martinez had been listening to the radio, had it jammed up against his right ear. 'But no sightings yet.'

'No sense heading the same way then,' Sam said.

The storm was easing, the rain almost past as he took the *Windswept* around in a curve, and the sudden impulse to drive this fine boat at full power, just to get them to Joshua as fast as he could, was hard to resist, but common sense won, kept him slow and steady, because the weather notwithstanding, wherever their beautiful boy was, Sam would be damned if he was going to make one single extra wave that might put Joshua in even greater danger.

'The ocean.' Grace spoke suddenly, raising her voice to be heard above the engine. 'He's taken him out to sea.'

'Perhaps,' Sam said. 'Or he might have—'

'It's the ocean.' She was insistent.

'We'll get out there,' Sam said, 'but we have to take it slow.'

'I *know* it, Sam.' Grace's voice was shrill now. 'I don't know why, but I do.'

Sam took a look back at her, could see her eyes, almost wild, in the light from Martinez's flashlight.

'Better get out there, man,' his partner said, having learned through the years, same as Sam, to trust Grace's intuition.

His radio clamoured and he lifted it to his ear again, screwing up his face, trying to listen.

'What?' Sam asked.

'Suspicious activity at Flamingo Marina a few hours ago.' Martinez spoke fast, keeping pace with what the dispatcher was reporting. 'Disturbance on a cruiser moored there.'

'What time?' asked Sam.

'Around two a.m.' – Martinez went on listening – 'and not the first time it's happened.' His dark eyes glinted with anger and frustration, because it had taken the fucking idiot witness so much time to call it in. 'Boat got taken out a while back,' he said. 'It's an old white Baja cruiser name of *Baby*.'

'Where's Flamingo?' Grace wanted to know.

'South of Belle Island,' Martinez said. 'If it's him, the bastard could have been cruising right by us when he called.'

Right under their noses, maybe, beneath Broad Causeway or even closer, beneath Kane Concourse, heading under Collins Avenue through Haulover out into the Atlantic.

'He might have gone south, not north,' Grace said.

Sam shook his head. 'He'd never go through Government Cut, not with the Coast Guard Station right on top of him.'

They heard the sound then.

Raucously loud and welcome.

'Chopper.' Martinez looked skyward.

'How did Miller say I make this goddamned boat go real fast?' Sam called over his shoulder.

'Just push the throttle forward.' Martinez leaned forward, pointed at the lever. 'Further you push it, the faster we go.'

Grace shut her eyes and said a swift prayer.

Sam pushed the throttle all the way.

The *Windswept* roared into life.

102

The helicopter sounded to Cal like the wrath of God.

Not long now.

He didn't know *how* it would go from here on, just that it would go.

The terror had receded again, because some things were meant to be, and there was no fighting them.

Some people were meant to die.

And if his hell was going to be Jewel, at least Cal knew it probably wouldn't be that much worse than too much of his life had been.

Not going back to jail – that much he'd decided.

No way.

103

The waters in Haulover were rougher than they'd anticipated, Sam riding the power-boat too fast, Grace and Martinez both hanging on as waves pounded and rocked the *Windswept*, but the three friends on board were way beyond caring for themselves, their goal, they hoped and prayed, somewhere out in that ocean up ahead, the expanse of darkness now starting to become more easily definable from the lighter grey, early dawn sky.

They could hear two choppers up there now, both getting louder, their lights visible, one ahead to the east, the other still farther north.

The radio began to crackle again, and Martinez jammed it tight against his right ear, struggling to hear.

'They've seen the cruiser,' he yelled.

'Where?' Sam yelled back as they roared out into the open Atlantic waters.

'What's *that*?' Grace had let go of the rail, was straining now to see through the binoculars, leaning forward, her heart thumping hard, her body wedged tightly against the side of the boat to give her better balance. 'Straight ahead.'

'That's *it*,' Martinez shouted. 'Has to be.'

They all saw it. A small white cruiser a couple of miles ahead, due east.

Motionless, it seemed, rocking in the water.

Windswept still pounding on.

'Need to start slowing down, man,' Martinez told Sam.

'Sam, slow *down*,' Grace yelled.

He was already throttling back, the boat responding swiftly.

Coming to get you, Joshua.

He was aware of other boats on their way, coming from north and south, aware of light and sound and movement on the waters, everyone coming to help, and the crackle from the radio was constant now.

'Maybe we should leave it to the Coast Guard,' Martinez yelled.

Knowing, sure as snakes spat, that Sam would not do that.

104

Baby was dead in the water now.

Going nowhere.

This old cruiser had seen a lot of living, Cal figured.

And dying, too.

No place left to go.

Time.

105

They were about a quarter of a mile away now, and Sam had the *Windswept* all the way down to a crawl.

'Al, take over,' he called, dragging off his shoes.

'What the fuck you doin', man?' Martinez stepped up and grabbed the wheel.

'Going to get our son.' Sam was already at the side, clambering up.

'Sam, I don't *know*.' Grace grabbed at his arm.

And then she let it go again, her thoughts suddenly crystal clear, knowing damned well that if he weren't heading overboard, she would be.

'Please be careful,' she told him. 'I need you both back.'

Martinez glanced up at the chopper, could see its green and white markings, almost overhead now. 'Better get off if you're going, man.'

And Sam took his dive.

He was halfway there when the world erupted.

He felt the shockwaves pound his body and reverberate in his head, ripping through ocean and air, dragging him under for too many long, horrible moments, and then he came up again, choking and coughing up salt water.

He could see stars in the sky, fiery stars everywhere.

Not stars at all.

'*Joshua*!' he screamed.

Too deafened by the explosion even to hear his own voice.

'*Sam*!' Grace screamed.

'Jesus,' Martinez said, feeling *Windswept* rocking and rolling beneath them, wondering abruptly if there might be more to come, if he should be taking Grace away from here.

And then the powerboat began to settle.

A curious kind of silence hung heavily in the air.

'I can't *see* anything!' Grace cried, because the smoke was like thick fog.

'*Sam*!' Martinez yelled.

The smoke cleared a little, shifted by the breeze.

They were both at the side, close together, peering through, struggling to see.

'Jesus Christ,' Martinez said, quite softly.

Because the *Baby* had gone.

Fragments and shards and atoms of Lord knew what else were still descending in an eerie slow kind of rain, settling on the surface of the water.

'Joshua!' Grace screamed. 'Sam!'

She moved suddenly, scrambling up, trying to get a hold, wanting to get over the side and into the water.

'No!' Martinez grabbed her round the waist.

'Let me *go*!'

'I can't do that.'

And then he saw.

'There!' he yelled. 'Sam's *there*!'

Grace froze, seeing him too, his dark head there one minute, mouth open, gulping air, then diving again.

Realization hit Martinez first.

'Oh, Jesus,' he said.

Because there was nothing left to dive for.

'Joshua,' Grace said, her voice very quiet, just before she folded at the waist and started to go down.

Martinez caught her.

It had been a long while since he had wept.

Sam, coming up for the fifth time, his heart exploding with grief and rage, saw it before the radio dispatcher reported the sighting from the helicopter.

'Dinghy north-east.'

Baby Moses.

He trod water for a moment, gasping for air, rubbing salt out of his eyes, lost his bearings, frantically twisted and turned in the water.

'Where'd it go?!' he yelled.

'There!' Martinez's voice was hoarse but loud enough, just reaching Sam over the noise of the chopper and the waves. 'To your left, man!'

On board the *Windswept*, Grace heard his voice, dragged herself up off the deck, shook away the dizziness, saw the dinghy, saw Sam almost there.

'Oh, my God,' she said. 'Oh, please God.'

Sam's eyes were stinging and the wounds on his chest were burning up.

Best pain he'd ever felt in his *life*.

Almost there. Two more strokes of his arms and his right hand touched rubber, then a kind of handle, grabbed hold.

'Joshua, I'm here, son.'

He began to haul himself up, knowing he had to be careful, terrified of causing a capsize, started to slide off again, heard Grace's voice cry out in fear, managed to hold on, get a firmer grip.

He saw the wicker basket.

With Joshua inside.

Best sight he'd ever seen.

His son's dark eyes were wide open, gazing calmly at his father.

'Thank you, sweet Jesus,' Sam said.

And scrambled into the dinghy.

106

'Tough little kid,' one of the doctors at Miami General told Sam and Grace with something like admiration.

They kept him in the hospital for observation – and because Dr David Becket, whose opinions they respected, had made a forceful request that they err on the side of caution – yet Joshua, remarkably, seemed little the worse for his ordeal, picking up quickly despite the antihistamine that Cooper had put into his system and the time – however long it had been – that he had spent in that dinghy.

His parents had never been so grateful for the warmth of Florida nights.

Jerome Cooper was gone, along with *Baby*, the most likely theory, shared by all concerned in the hunt, that he had probably chosen to end his lousy life along with the cruiser, possibly inspired by the youthful Bang Gang, by stuffing a rag in the boat's gasoline tank and igniting it.

One grisly piece of evidence had been swiftly found in the debris: human remains still to be officially identified. Part of a woman's finger with a white-polished nail, yielding the strong probability that Roxanne Lucca – who they now knew had flown from Chicago to Miami just a little ahead of Sam – had been on board with Cooper when *Baby* had exploded.

Mother and son both missing, presumed dead.

No one on earth, so far as the Beckets knew, mourning their loss.

'I'm so glad Jerome's dead,' Grace told Claudia on the phone on Thursday evening, calling her from the paediatric floor. 'I'd be afraid, otherwise, of what Sam might want to do to him.'

Miami General calling Westlake Hospital in Melrose Park, where Claudia was still doing what little she could for their father.

'I'm sure Sam would leave it to justice,' Claudia said.

'Maybe it's me then I'm not so sure about,' said Grace.

'I wish I was back there with you,' Claudia said.

'Don't you think it's about time you went back home, sis?'

'If Dan still wants me.'

'Just get back there and find out,' Grace said.

107

June 20

Mildred was doing much better.

Sam had been doing his best to visit with her most days, his father standing in for him when his son couldn't make it in.

'She's a very special lady,' David agreed with Sam.

'She seems quite taken with you, too,' said Sam.

Eight days had passed since the abduction, and Grace had roasted two chickens in honour of Friday night, Saul taking his turn – Becket family style – to light the Sabbath candles. And right now, dinner over, Saul was in the kitchen, washing up, while Grace was upstairs in the nursery, checking up on Joshua for the fifth time since they'd sat down at the table.

The older father and son were out on the deck, Woody – given the all-clear less than a day after his own ordeal – lying contentedly at Sam's feet on the planks.

'Has Mildred mentioned her plans after she's discharged?' David wanted to know.

'She surely can't go back to living rough.'

'I think we'll have a tough time talking her out of it,' Sam said.

'Maybe it's up to us then,' his father said, slowly, 'to come up with some kind of workable alternative.'

Sam was intrigued. 'What kind of alternative?'

'Give me time,' said David.

108

June 23

Elliot Sanders gave Sam a call at the office the following Monday morning.

'I thought I should tell you myself,' he said.

'What now?' Much as he appreciated the doc, Sam had found over the years that he seldom had cause to enjoy calls from medical examiners.

'There was only one body on the *Baby*,' Sanders said. 'There's a whole lot of stuff it's going to take a long time to sift through and analyse, but every piece of flesh and bone and tooth spared by that explosion belonged to the mother.'

'No trace of Cooper at all?' Sam asked.

It wasn't the first frustration to grate on the

detectives since the killer's probable death. Martinez had uncovered, just days ago, a rap sheet for Cooper that had been misfiled because of someone's spelling mistake – and if Sam had found that prison record right after Jerome's visit to their house, he'd have gotten an arrest warrant then and there, and the second victim might have been saved and Joshua would not have been taken.

'Human fucking error,' Martinez had said.

'Has to happen once in a while,' Sam had said, more calmly than he'd felt.

'Yeah,' Martinez had said. 'Shit happens.'

Cold, hard proof of Cooper's guilt in the killings was still in maddeningly short supply. They had established that *Baby* had been sold to him in Wilmington, North Carolina, and the witness who had reported the disturbance on the cruiser had also identified the man he'd seen a few times at the marina as Jerome Cooper.

'There's no real doubt,' Sanders continued now on the phone, 'that Cooper was on the boat prior to the blast, but we simply have nothing to prove that he was still on board when it went up.'

Spectres danced before Sam's mind's eye.

Silver angels of death.

'But this isn't the final word, right?' he asked.

'Not officially, no,' Sanders said, 'but as good as.' The ME paused. 'I'm sorry, Sam. I wish I had something more conclusive for you.'

'Me too,' Sam said.

109

June 29

'The sonofabitch has gotta be dead,' Martinez said almost a week later.

Not certain, even as he spoke, that it was the truth.

Just wanting it to be so.

Missing, presumed drowned.

Cooper had been seen taking the *Baby* out of Flamingo Marina, was almost certainly the individual who'd stuffed the rag into the gasoline tank – and the chances of his diving overboard at that point and escaping were remote, given that the explosion would have occurred as soon as the naked flame had hit the fumes from the open tank. The consensus of opinion, therefore, was that if he had by chance survived, with so many boats out there at the time, someone would surely have spotted Cooper swimming away. And if he'd tried coming ashore in the first several hours after that, chances were that he'd have been caught and charged.

Chances.

'What we need,' Sam said now, 'is a body.'

He'd lost count of the number of times he'd said that.

Not just for them. For the Adani family and the second victim, still nameless.

'Ocean's a big place, man,' said Martinez.

'Not good enough,' said Sam. 'Not nearly good enough.'

110

July 1

Still no second body, but there had been a major breakthrough in the homicide investigation, after one José Ricardo, the manager of a bed and breakfast on Collins Avenue in South Beach, had discovered that one of his employees had been renting out a space at the back of his building.

No name for the tenant, cash changing hands, his employee since fired.

But the occupant had left a small stack of notebooks filled with writing.

'I was going to throw them in the trash,' Ricardo had told the MBPD officers who'd first responded to his phone call, 'but then I took a closer look and figured you might be interested.'

Sam Becket and Alejandro Martinez had been more than interested.

The writings of the killer had filled five and a half books, all with the same title.

'The Epistle of Cal the Hater'.

An all but unrecognizable individual, hard for the most part to reconcile with the weak young man who'd shown up at the Becket house that morning three weeks ago, but still Jerome Cooper beyond a shadow of a doubt – his sadistic, racist mother referred to as 'Jewel' most of the time, but identified as Roxanne or Roxy once or twice.

Sam Becket mentioned, too.

And the hate that 'Cal' had felt for him.

The 'epistles' would be studied for a long time to come.

Which would – that much was abundantly, sickeningly clear to Sam and Martinez – have pleased the madman himself.

111

Claudia and Daniel had been in Chicago for three days, staying at the Hyatt Regency, when Sam and Grace flew into O'Hare.

The Brownleys had come because Frank would soon be ready to leave hospital, and neither Claudia nor Daniel, having been reconciled, had wanted any more time apart. A nursing home had already been chosen, and the Melrose Park house – no longer a crime scene – was to be put up for sale.

Grace and Sam had come down in time for the Fourth, joining them at the hotel and watching the fireworks together at the Navy Pier.

David and Saul were back home, taking fine care of Joshua, and David was in dogged ongoing negotiations with Mildred Bleeker, trying to persuade her to come stay with him for a period of convalescence after her discharge from Miami General.

'Negotiating Middle East peace might be easier,' David had told Sam last week.

'No pushover, our Mildred,' Sam had said.

'I did warn you.'

'She's a proud lady. I respect that.'

'Which just might be the one thing that lets her give in,' Sam had said.

'Pride?' His father had looked dubious.

'I meant your respect,' Sam had said.

It was the first time Grace had seen Frank in more than seven years.

Some of the old hatred melting away beneath pity for his helplessness.

'Not such a bad feeling,' she told Sam afterwards. 'Shedding a little bitterness.'

'Poor old guy,' said Sam.

'Let's not go overboard,' Grace said.

They all went together to close up the house.

The posters had been taken off the walls in Jerome's room.

Still more than enough left to give Sam and Claudia chills.

There was nothing in the place that either of the sisters wanted to take away for any kind of remembrance. Enough bad memories left over from their years in the first Lucca house to last them a lifetime.

'How about we all get out of here?' Daniel said when they'd done. 'I don't know about you guys, but I could use a stiff drink.'

'Sounds like a plan to me,' Sam said.

'So what are we waiting for?' said Grace.

The New Epistle of Cal the Hater

I watched them go into my house.

One big happy family.

The kind that drove Jewel crazy.

And then a while later I watched Detective Becket shake the real estate guy's hand.

Doing their deal, I guess.

Not so much as a backward glance when they all left.

The FOR SALE sign went up outside less than two hours later.

Stealing my home, my possessions.

Same way they've taken or spoiled everything else.

And made me destroy the only thing I had left.

I miss my *Baby* a whole lot.

And Daisy, too, come to that.

I read the other day that Jerome Cooper is missing, presumed drowned.

Cooper's dead, all right.

But not Cal the Hater.

Cal is very much alive.

Cal knows how to change his appearance.

And how to earn enough to get by.

Cal the Hater has plans. To come back some time and get what's his.

And get even, too.

Count on it, Samuel Lincoln Becket.